Copyright © 2019 by Archimedes Books. All rights reserved.

No part of this book may be reproduced, scanned, or distributed in any printed or electronic form without permission. Please do not participate in or encourage piracy of copyrighted materials in violation of the author's rights. Thank you for respecting the hard work of this author.

This is a work of fiction. Names, characters, places, and incidents either are the product of the author's imagination or are used fictitiously, and any resemblance to locales, events, business establishments, or actual persons— living or dead—is entirely coincidental.

ABSOLUTION

FORSAKEN MERCENARY BOOK TWO

JONATHAN YANEZ

CONTENTS

Books in the Forsaken Mercenary Universe — vii
Stay Informed — ix

Chapter One — 1
Chapter Two — 13
Chapter Three — 23
Chapter Four — 33
Chapter Five — 45
Chapter Six — 55
Chapter Seven — 67
Chapter Eight — 79
Chapter Nine — 89
Chapter Ten — 99
Chapter Eleven — 109
Chapter Twelve — 121
Chapter Thirteen — 133
Chapter Fourteen — 143
Chapter Fifteen — 151
Chapter Sixteen — 163
Chapter Seventeen — 175
Chapter Eighteen — 185
Chapter Nineteen — 195
Chapter Twenty — 205
Chapter Twenty-One — 219
Chapter Twenty-Two — 229
Chapter Twenty-Three — 237
Chapter Twenty-Four — 253
Chapter Twenty-Five — 263
Chapter Twenty-Six — 271
Chapter Twenty-Seven — 281

Chapter Twenty-Eight	293
Epilogue	303
Stay Informed	313
Books in the Forsaken Mercenary Universe	315

BOOKS IN THE FORSAKEN MERCENARY UNIVERSE

Inception

Dropship

Absolution

Fury

Vendetta

Annihilation

Nemesis

Rivals

Wolves

Crusade

Traitor

Parabellum

Judgment

STAY INFORMED

Get A Free Book by visiting Jonathan Yanez' website.

You can email me at jonathan.alan.yanez@gmail.com or find me on Facebook and Instagram (@author_jonathan_yanez). I also created a special Facebook group called "Jonathan's Reading Wolves" specifically for readers, where I reveal new cover art, do giveaways, and run contests. Please check it out and join whenever you get the chance!

For updates about new releases, as well as exclusive promotions, join the VIP mailing list. Head there now to receive a free copy of *Inception*.

STAY INFORMED

jonathan-yanez.com

Enjoying the series? Help others discover the beginning of the *Forsaken Mercenary* series by sharing with a friend.

CHAPTER ONE

JUST LIKE THAT, my world was plunged from some kind of stability into chaos once more. The cell room in the secret Phoenix base I was in, speaking with Echo, was plunged into darkness. The emergency lights kicked on.

The Phoenix guards near the door of the cell block spoke nervously into their comm units.

"What's going on out there?" one of them inquired with a quivering voice.

"Commander Shaw, orders?" the other asked into her earpiece.

"You should really let me out of here," Echo said, reclining on his bunk as if he didn't have a care in the world. "What's coming for you now is far worse than anything you've faced before. You can trust me on that one, Danny."

I eyed Echo without smiling. My right hand went to the small of my back where my MK II should have rested. I had left it in my quarters when I came down to see Echo. I didn't think I'd need it. It wasn't the first time I'd been wrong, and it wouldn't be the last.

"X, can you get us connected to the comm channel they're operating on?" I asked as the two Phoenix guards looked at one another uneasily then glanced my way. "Or maybe they'll just give it to us."

"Tune in to channel two, five, seven, point three, five, nine," the female Phoenix guard said. "You'll be able to hear what's going on out there."

"Tuning in now," X said inside of my head.

"—All units are to maintain your positions," Commander Shaw said without a hint of fear in his voice. "All off-duty personnel are ordered to report to your commanding officers in full gear immediately."

"They don't know what's coming for them," Echo said in a laugh. "None of you do. You're all going to die. Except for you, Danny, because you're a survivor."

"Shut up!" the male Phoenix guard barked. He looked over at me. His eyes were wide with a mixture of worry and anger. "Shut him up!"

"Wait." The female guard took a step closer to

Echo's cell, the blaster she held in her hands pointed down. Her pointer finger hovered over the trigger. "Who's coming? Tell us what's happening."

I wasn't sure if it was the small room or the fact that the main lights were out and we were bathed in the dull blue backup lights, but a cold chill touched the base of my spine.

Should have brought your MK II with you, I berated myself. *You know better.*

I studied the room as Echo began his story. There was one way in and one way out, a closed door in front of us with a circular viewport. The room was large enough for three cells. Echo was the only one staying in one now. The light blue force field that kept him secured hummed with a distinct buzz.

"Immortal Corp is just one of the many private firms in the galaxy," Echo said with a sigh as if he were teaching children and class was in session. "There are dozens of others, some small, others mid-size, with unlimited resources at their disposal. But the one that's here now, The Order. They're the major players. The real deal. They're the only other private corporation that holds a candle to Immortal Corp."

The room went quiet.

"If they're here now, and they've sent Cyber Hunters, it's already over." Echo shrugged. "Your best bet is to put yourselves into one of these cells and try to break the locking mechanism so it can't be turned off when you're in there."

"Rose, he's lying," the male Phoenix guard said. "He's lying to scare us."

"No, no, Mark," Rose said. "I don't think he is."

"It's confirmed we have a breach and enemies inside the Vault," Commander Shaw said through the comms. "Our main generators have been sabotaged. The base is on lockdown. I'm sending reinforcements to secure the prisoner and Monica Warden along with the super seed. Eyes open. We'll find who's here if we have to go floor by floor."

The two guards must have had various channels open, able to receive incoming communication. While my comm was silent, I could see Rose and Mark stand up straight as new orders came via their earpieces.

"Yes, sir," Mark said. He eyed me, gripping his rifle tightly in his hands. Being an ancient weapons enthusiast, the rifle reminded me of pictures I had seen of a M4 carbine. His weapon was silver and bulkier, but it carried a similar shape. "Understood."

I felt my heart rate pick up in speed as Mark and Rose both looked in my direction. They came at me in angles to cut off my path to the door. The animal inside, I was still understanding, was eager for the fight.

Before I could throw the first punch, Mark handed me his sidearm, grip first.

"It's not that hand cannon of yours, but it'll have to do for now," Mark said, offering me the weapon. "Commander Shaw said to make sure you were armed."

"He said you can be trusted," Rose chimed in. She leveled her stare at me, unflinching. "Can you be trusted?"

I accepted the lightweight weapon that felt so small in my hands compared to my MK II.

"I'm not going to shoot you in the back if that's what you're trying to get at," I answered. "We're in this together. Whatever this is."

"Cyber Hunters," Echo said with an exasperated sigh. "Are you people even listening to me? I swear, if Phoenix is this far out of the know, you have zero chance of surviving what's about to happen. I—"

Rose went to the side of Echo's cell and pressed a button on the control panel that dampened the sound coming from his cell.

"Thank you," Mark said with a sigh of his own. "I was about to do that or put a round in his head.

Although I'm not sure that would have done much good anyway."

"X?" I asked loud enough the other two could hear. "Can you shed some light for us on these Cyber Hunters?"

"Certainly," X said over her external speakers so Mark and Rose could hear as well. Although her speakers were limited to the small circular disk on the right side of my neck just behind my ear, they were loud enough to fill a room. "The Cyber Hunters are more myth than fact, as is the Order, for that matter."

I listened intently at the information X relayed to us, looking over at Echo from time to time. He hadn't moved from his position by his bunk. The skin and flesh over his face was still healing. Half of his face looked normal, the other a combination of muscle and ligaments growing over a bone-white skull.

"The Order has been linked to many names in the past, including The Knights Templar and the Illuminati. The Order is attributed to aiding in Earth's downfall; however, these facts have never been confirmed," X explained. She paused here more for our own sanity than the fact that she needed to catch her breath. "Cyber Hunters are robotically enhanced soldiers said to have been used by the Order to achieve various objectives over the years. None have ever been caught alive. The only thing known about them at all is through stories and the random carcasses found after an altercation."

"Daniel, is this you?" Monica's familiar voice sounded in my ear. "I saw the 'X' call sign over the shared channel and thought it might be."

"I'm here," I said, turning my head to the side. "Are you okay?"

"I'll be fine," Monica said in a hushed whisper. "I'm in the lab working on the super seed. Commander Shaw has a company of soldiers here. Nothing's going to get us. I—"

The channel went to static.

"Monica?" I asked, already knowing she wasn't coming back. "Monica, can you hear me? Monica?"

Nothing.

Mark and Rose looked at me for direction.

That was definitely the wrong thing to do. I wasn't a leader. I couldn't even remember what I was. Before I had to answer their questioning looks, a figure passed by the door.

My neck snapped to the circular viewport that separated this room from the hall outside. I was too slow to see who or what it was. The lighting was too poor. The only thing I knew for certain was that who or whatever passed by the door was fast.

"Someone's at the door," I said, lifting the blaster in my hands toward the door. "They're here."

Rose and Mark ran to each side of the door, slamming their shoulders into the wall. They pointed their heavy blasters toward the door.

"Is anyone near the prisoner's cell level?" Rose asked over the comms. "I repeat, are there any friendlies outside the cell level?"

"That's affirmative," a tough male voice said over the open channel. "I'm coming under order of Commander Shaw to help in securing the prisoner."

"Robert," Mark said with a sigh of relief. "We could use some support. It's good to hear your voice."

"We're right down the hall. We see the cell door—what the—I…" Robert's voice was drowned out in a hail of weapons fire that boomed right outside of our cell door.

Screams of the dead and dying echoed into our room.

"We have to go and help," I said, marching toward the door. "They're here."

"No," Mark said, shaking his head emphatically. "We have our orders just like they do. We secure the prisoner."

I looked at Rose. All the blood drained from her

face. Her hands shook as she gripped her weapon tighter.

"Well, I guess that's why I'll never make a good soldier ," I said, placing my hand on the door handle. "I've never been one to do what I'm told."

I was not sure if Mark was going to let me out or put the barrel of his weapon in my belly and order me to stay. We'd never find out.

The screaming outside as well as the sound of weapons being discharged quieted. One second, the noise sounded as though people were yelling in a thunderstorm, the next, dead still.

Something struck the steel door so hard, it made an indention on our side of the barrier. The indention looked like the crude shape of a fist.

The blow came again. We all moved away from the door and pointed our weapons at the metal slab we foolishly thought would keep us safe.

Three more hits came in rapid succession and I knew it wouldn't take another.

I could see Echo to my left. My peripheral vision told me he was on his feet yelling something at us. What, we couldn't hear, but I could bet he was offering his help if we let him out.

The door came down with another savage blow. I

stood sideways with my weapon out in front of me. Aiming at this close a range wouldn't be difficult.

A figure dressed in black stood in the doorway. He or she—I couldn't be sure yet—stood staring at us through the shadow of a deep black hood.

"S-stop," Mark said, finding his voice in the tense moment. "Surrender now or you'll be shot."

The figure remained silent. Instead of answering, it stepped into the room. I could see it was a woman now. The poor lighting in our room made it impossible to make out distinct features of her face, but inside of the hood, I think she wore a mask.

"The lighting's bad. I'm not sure if your night vision will help, but you can try," X reminded me in my head.

I kicked myself for not thinking of it sooner. I concentrated on it, then blinked. The room went from a dark glowing blue to a golden glow as my enhanced vision aided my sight. It still wasn't enough to see the woman's face in the deep hood, but it made the room brighter, and right now, I would take any advantage I could get.

"Stop right now!" Rose shouted as the figure took another step into the room.

"Screw this," I said out loud, opening fire with my

handgun. Red bolts of energy streaked across the room toward my target.

She was fast, impossibly fast. The black clad figure sprinted toward us on the right side of the room. A shield opened up like a fan on her right forearm.

Rose and Mark opened fire. I was sure I hit her a half dozen times, but the rounds landed on the shield she opened, not on her skull or torso where I aimed.

Mark's and Rose's rounds went wild, some hitting the shield, most scorching the wall. The Cyber Hunter leaped off the ground, sprinting the last few strides on the wall itself.

By the time I switched up my strategy to try and aim for the Cyber Hunter's legs, it was too late. She was on top of us.

CHAPTER TWO

A PAIR of foot-long blades sprouted from the back of her left arm, much like the shield had opened from her right.

She impaled Rose with her first strike. At the same time, the cloaked woman swiped with her shield arm at my head, slicing sideways she used her shield as a secondary weapon instead of a defensive object.

I ducked, rolling out of the way. I came up with my firearm ready. The assassin flung Rose's body to the side, twirling toward Mark.

I sent a burst of weapon fire at her. My rounds hit her this time. I knew at least one round struck something vital. The Cyber Hunter hesitated for a moment then continued the assault on Mark, taking his head from his shoulders with a single swipe of her circular shield.

I emptied my clip at her, more out of anger at how easily she had just killed the two Phoenix guards than anything else.

What a day to leave your MK II, Daniel, I shouted at myself in my head. *What a day.*

The handgun in my palm clicked dry. I stood up from my crouched position as the Cyber Hunter circled me. The deep hood she wore on her shoulders fell back from her face. Like I had expected, she wore a mask underneath.

The mask was black like the rest of what she wore. As far as I could tell, there were no eyepieces for her to see through, neither were there a nose hole nor a mouth.

The only thing that broke the plain blank darkness of her mask at all was a crimson red cross on the forehead, nearly too dark to tell what it was. The cross carried another smaller parallel mark right under the first.

"You're not like them," a hard female voice said through the cloth over her face. She motioned down to the ground where Mark's and Rose's still bodies lay. "You're not like them at all. You're something different."

We circled each other slowly. I searched her body to see where the round that made it through had struck her. The black robe she wore made it impossible to see where she was vulnerable. What I did see was a tiny trickle of blood and something black coming off her left side. The black liquid looked like some kind of fluid you'd use in a machine.

"I'm not the only one that's different," I said, motioning to the liquid sprinkled on the ground like a faint mist in the early morning. "What do you want?"

"There's a storm coming," she said, ignoring my question. "I don't know who or what you are, but you're in the wrong place at the wrong time."

"I've been through a few storms in my day," I told her. "As far as being in the wrong place at the wrong time, story of my life."

"I can see everything you're seeing through your eyes," X said in my head. "Her weapons are detachable, be careful."

I wasn't sure how X knew that just by looking at them, but I wasn't going to argue.

Sensing I was buying time for some kind of advantage in the fight, the woman dressed in black lunged at me with her blades on her left arm and her shield on her right.

She was quick, but so was I. I ducked the swipe

from her blades. They whistled past my head as hardened steel came within inches of my hair. She struck out with her shield, positioning it sideways to decapitate me like she had Mark. I leaned back to avoid the blow then lunged in close to take the fight to her.

I landed a left hook to her face, followed by a right uppercut. Whoever this chick was, she was one tough cookie. I felt her absorb the blows with not so much as a grunt before pivoting to grab me by my waist and toss me over her hip.

I landed in a roll in time to see her shield in a direct line for my head. Already on my knees, I leaned back to allow the steel disc to sail over my face. It clanked against the ground behind me, ricocheting into the master panel in charge of controlling Echo's cell. A shower of sparks followed.

"Let me out!" Echo screamed as the noise dampeners to his cell failed. "Let me out! I can help! No matter what's happened in the past, we're still united against the Order or have you forgotten all of that too?"

The woman in black looked over at Echo and then back at me. She cocked her head to the side as if seeing me for the first time.

"Ahhh, that makes sense. The puppy that was lost

has been found again," she crooned. "And you don't remember a thing?"

I slowly rose to my feet. Maybe I was crazy, but for the first time, I was actually thinking of letting Echo out. I could match my assailant for speed, but she tossed me over her hip like I threw old shirts into the hamper.

There was a clear differential in strength.

"What is it that you want?" I asked again, buying as much time as I could. "Why are you here?"

"I was here for him." The woman motioned to Echo with her chin. "But now that I know two of you are here, I guess I'm here for you as well."

"Listen, lady," I said, taking a small step forward with my hands out in front of me. I positioned my right foot just under Mark's rifle. "I don't know who you are, what this Order is, or why you want Echo dead, but I don't blame you. I don't like him either and I just met him."

"Wait, what?" Echo screamed from his cell in pure mania. "Daniel, she's our enemy. She's our sworn enemy."

"Maybe yours," I said to Echo without taking my eyes off the faceless woman. "I had no quarrel with you."

"'Had'." The woman repeated the word.

"That's right," I said. "You killed these Phoenix guards who were just doing their job. It doesn't seem right to let you walk out of here now."

"Like you could stop me," the woman said in a voice that told me she was smiling under that black mask. "But that's sweet in a heroic kind of way. Too bad I have to kill you now. You seem like a nice guy."

"You don't know me that well," I said.

We moved at once. She lunged at me with the two-bladed weapon coming out of the top of her left forearm.

At that same time, I kicked up violently with my right knee. The rifle that had been just on top of my foot lifted into the air with the motion. I grabbed it and lit into the approaching woman a moment faster than she could cut the weapon in two.

Two rounds hit her in the arm and chest before she sliced the blaster in half. She cracked me across the jaw with her left fist then slammed her right fist toward me.

The twin blades of her weapon came for my gut. I twisted out of the way but not before she took a slice out of me that made me gasp in pain. Cold steel sliced through my side.

I grunted, ignoring the pain and looking past the agony to the opening she had given me by overextending her reach. I slammed my own fist into her stomach as hard as I could.

Finally, I was rewarded with a reaction that actually sounded like I did some kind of damage to her. In the second it took her to recover, I ripped off the black mask hiding her face.

A curtain of jet black hair fell over her eyes. The only way I could describe her was violently beautiful.

She recovered, slashing at my head before twirling to the side and ripping her shield out of the control panel that held Echo in place.

To both of our surprise, the panel exploded in another shower of sparks. The blue force field holding Echo inside disappeared.

The three of us circled one another as Echo exited his prison, his half skull, half regular face grinning. Height and width wise, he was larger than either of us. We made quite a trio, the dark-haired beauty, the grinning half skull face, and me.

"Do I have to worry about you right now?" Echo asked me without taking his eyes off the woman. "Can we put our differences aside for a moment?"

I almost said yes. I almost agreed to let the man who murdered the woman I loved have a free pass. I wish I could remember more and actually feel the hate for him I knew I should, but I didn't. I just had to react as I knew I would if I did remember.

"I can't do that," I told him. "Not after what you confessed to. Not after what you did to her."

Echo sneered, looking at me now. He took a step farther back to try and take me and the dark-haired woman in at once.

"My, my," the woman said, clicking her teeth. "I came at an interesting time in Immortal Corp politics."

"Daniel," X said in my head. "If you can keep them talking a few more minutes, I have word that an entire platoon of Phoenix soldiers are on their way here. I've kept the chatter quiet so you can concentrate."

"Thanks," I said, making the mistake of saying it out loud. "Sorry, I do that. Talk to myself sometimes. I'm not right in the head."

Echo and the dark-haired woman looked at me as though they didn't believe me in the slightest.

The woman made the first move before I could try and make another excuse. The next few seconds were a definition of pain and reflexes. I dodged blows from both Echo and the dark-haired woman as I traded strikes with them and they did the same with one another.

It was every man and woman for themselves. I had a cut open over my forehead by an elbow from Echo and my lips split as I was bashed with the woman's shield.

Within that short time, Echo was limping and dark liquid poured from the woman's nose. It wasn't blood, but something else, like that dark hue of motor oil that still sprinkled from her side.

We probably would have kept at it if it weren't for the shouting coming from the hall. The Phoenix reinforcements had arrived.

Without hesitation, the woman reached into her cloak, slamming a trio of small glass balls on the ground. With a hiss, the room was covered in white gas that brought tears to my eyes. The gas entered my throat, filling my lungs with its stinging acrid taste.

I tried in vain to stem the gas entering my mouth and nose. I buried my face in the crook of my elbow, retreating to the back of the room where the gas was less likely to choke me.

I could hear more shouting as the Phoenix guards entered the room. The gas was so thick and the lights still too dull to see much.

"Here, I've got one here." One of the guards coughed, approaching me through the gas with a handkerchief over his face. "No, no, it's one of ours, not the prisoner."

"There, there's a woman too with dark hair. She

was just here," I said, coughing even more. A new wave of tears swam past my eyes. "They were both just here."

"There was no one here but you when we came into the room," Commander Shaw said, appearing out of the smoke. He shoved a handkerchief at me.

"Thanks." I coughed into the handkerchief. "You have Echo and a Cyber Hunter running free through your facility. Here, look!"

I crouched down, looking at the ground and the trail of oil splatter that led into the corridor.

Commander Shaw turned to bark orders to his men.

I was already out the door.

"Who would you like to find first?" X asked out loud. "I can recommend levels to search based on the idea that Echo is trying to escape and the Cyber Hunter is going after him."

"Not yet," I told X. "Weapons first."

CHAPTER THREE

MY MIND RACED with ideas as I entered the small quarters provided for me back at the Vault. The lights in the Vault clicked on at the same time. Apparently, someone had managed to fix whatever damage the Cyber Hunter had done to them. I concentrated on turning my enhanced vision off. Like magic, I could see normally again.

Still have to get used to being able to see in the dark by just willing myself to, I thought to myself.

The room was small with nothing more than a bed, a dresser and an adjacent washroom.

I opened the top dresser drawer, taking my MK II in my hand like I was shaking the palm of an old friend. I placed the piece of steel at the small of my back.

"Should never have left you," I said out loud.

"Do I need to give you two a moment?" X asked. "I can turn off if you'd like."

Despite almost being killed by a Cyber Hunter, having lost our prisoner and everything else, I actually grinned.

"No, you're good, X," I said. "Any word on our escapees?"

"None, I've been monitoring the channel and—" X hesitated for a moment. "There's something going on at the hangar bay level."

X allowed the channel to play in my ear.

"We have contact in the hangar bay by the dropships!" a female voice I didn't recognize yelled out. "No sign of the Cyber Hunter, but we have the prisoner named Echo in our sights."

That was enough for me. I was off at a sprint.

"X, I need the fastest way to the hangar bay," I said.

"On it," X answered. A moment later, a broken yellow line appeared in front of me. I knew it was only X layering an augmented path for me to follow. I would have stopped to think how extraordinary this was a few days ago, but now it seemed things like seeing in the dark, Cyber Hunters, and voices in my head were the new normal.

I sprinted through the level, ignoring the lift and going straight for a set of stairs.

"The lift won't be faster?" I asked, breathing hard.

"The hangar bay is only five stories above us," X answered. "With the lifts in heavy use at the moment and the fact you can run faster than any normal human, the quickest route is the stairs."

It seemed we weren't the only ones that thought this. Phoenix guards jammed the stairwell running to the same floor.

"Hey, excuse me, coming through!" I shouted as I took the steps two at a time.

I'm not sure if they recognized me or it was the pure look of determination in my eyes, but they let me pass as I sprinted up the steps. Whatever Immortal Corp had done to me made me not only faster but gave me the ability to run without a normal level of fatigue setting in.

In seconds, I was up the five flights of stairs and bursting through the door to the hangar bay. Like most hangar bays, the room was gigantic. Dropships sat on the wide open floor with two massive hangar bay doors that opened out onto the side of the mountain.

Racks of gear and equipment lined the walls with high overhanging lights. There were more details to take in, but at the moment, I only had eyes for the scene playing out in front of me. There were four dropships in the hangar. They sat in a row with their rears towards us and cargo bay doors closed.

Echo held a grenade in his right hand, poised to detonate if he released the depressor. A group of Phoenix guards surrounded him as he yelled obscenities at them.

"Who wants to die!?" Echo was yelling. "Open the dropship now or we're all going up in flames together, except I'll come back. You won't."

"Get back!" I yelled as I reached for my MK II. I aimed the weapon at Echo, choosing an explosive magazine to jam into the butt of my weapon. "If any of you know who I am, trust me, and tell the other soldiers to get back."

The Phoenix guards looked to one another for consensus. The ones who had heard of me or seen me before nodded to the others. They all took a few steps back from Echo. Not one of them lowered their weapon.

"There he is." Echo looked at me with a smile. "Ready to go back home, Danny? We can both get on this—"

I probably shouldn't have. The Phoenix guards were far enough away and they all wore armor, but still, something could have gone wrong. I fired an explosive round at the grenade Echo held in his hand.

Both explosive devices detonated, flinging Echo into the side of the dropship so violently, when he struck the piece of equipment, I could hear bones snap. The Phoenix guards around him were blown back but seemed to have been able to avoid injury.

All I felt on my end was a wave of heat as the explosion took place too far away from me to do any real harm. I walked over the hangar floor unfazed. Echo lay on his stomach in a pool of his own blood. He didn't move, but I knew he wasn't dead. His clothes were charred, entire sections of his skin and flesh gone, but I knew what he was now.

"Daniel, Daniel, are you okay?" Monica asked, coming to a stop beside me. She wore a heavy chest plate and carried a rifle that she pointed down on Echo's still body.

"I'm fine," I said, motioning to Echo with my chin. "He's not."

Some captain or lieutenant, I wasn't really sure, got over his shock and started taking command of the situation. Echo was bound hand and foot and taken to a secure room.

Monica and I walked with Commander Shaw, who

arrived a few minutes later to see that Echo was properly secured.

"We haven't been able to find the Cyber Hunter, but the entire Vault is on high alert." Commander Shaw rubbed his red eyes. "If I had to put money on it, he's gone. The Cyber Hunter would be insane to stay here while we search the Vault for him."

"She." I corrected the commander, remembering the dark-haired woman who bled oil.

"What's that?" Commander Shaw asked, turning to me as we made our way to the lift and took it up a few stories.

"You keep referring to the Cyber Hunter as a 'he.' It was a woman," I said, shaking my head trying to describe her. "She wasn't entirely human either."

"I thought they were a myth," Monica said, narrowing her eyes as if that would help bring order to a situation in utter chaos. "I thought they were stories like a secret order in books. It can't be Cyber Hunters and the Order. They don't exist."

"Well, whoever that woman was took a chunk out of me," I said, looking down at the shirt that was torn on the side. My body had already healed, but the bloodstains were there. "She felt pretty real."

"I should level with you and tell you what—"

We both looked over at the commander as the

doors to the lift opened and a pair of Phoenix guards stood at attention. The commander closed his mouth. He nodded to the guards and continued down the level.

Whatever the commander was about to say was for our ears only. We followed him this time in silence. He directed us to a closed door on the right side of the hall.

Farther down, four heavily armored Phoenix guards stood at attention at another closed door.

We walked into the room, following Commander Shaw. As soon as we entered, I realized what it was. We stood in a small viewing room. In front of us was a one-way see-through wall.

In the room opposite us, Echo sat chained to a table. He was hunched over, still a mess of skin and flesh, but the bleeding had stopped. He might even be conscious now and only playing opossum. I wouldn't put that past him.

The small room we were in didn't offer much in the way of furniture. There were a few uncomfortable-looking chairs and a table pressed against one of the walls.

"All he sees on his end is another wall," Commander Shaw informed us. "The room is soundproof as well unless we decide otherwise."

"You were going to tell us something," I reminded the commander. Or maybe I didn't remind him and he decided not to tell us. Either way, I wasn't going to let it go now.

Commander Shaw eyed me and Monica for a long minute. I could practically see the gears turning behind his eyes as he decided exactly what to tell us and how much to let us know.

"Okay, okay," Commander Shaw said, pulling at his long grey beard. "You might want to sit down for this."

Monica and I took seats in the chairs. They were in fact as uncomfortable as they looked.

"Monica and her father have been working with Phoenix long enough that we have had the opportunity to build trust." Commander Shaw eyed me with a heavy sigh. "We haven't had that time, Daniel, but you don't get to where I am without learning how to read people. My gut tells me that I can trust you. That's why you were allowed to keep your weapon, that's why you have free rein in the Vault. So tell me. Am I right? Can I trust you?"

It almost seemed silly. Here he was looking at me asking if he could trust me when he already had. I think he knew the answer. He just wanted to hear it from me.

"Yes," I said. "You can trust me."

doors to the lift opened and a pair of Phoenix guards stood at attention. The commander closed his mouth. He nodded to the guards and continued down the level.

Whatever the commander was about to say was for our ears only. We followed him this time in silence. He directed us to a closed door on the right side of the hall.

Farther down, four heavily armored Phoenix guards stood at attention at another closed door.

We walked into the room, following Commander Shaw. As soon as we entered, I realized what it was. We stood in a small viewing room. In front of us was a one-way see-through wall.

In the room opposite us, Echo sat chained to a table. He was hunched over, still a mess of skin and flesh, but the bleeding had stopped. He might even be conscious now and only playing opossum. I wouldn't put that past him.

The small room we were in didn't offer much in the way of furniture. There were a few uncomfortable-looking chairs and a table pressed against one of the walls.

"All he sees on his end is another wall," Commander Shaw informed us. "The room is soundproof as well unless we decide otherwise."

"You were going to tell us something," I reminded the commander. Or maybe I didn't remind him and he decided not to tell us. Either way, I wasn't going to let it go now.

Commander Shaw eyed me and Monica for a long minute. I could practically see the gears turning behind his eyes as he decided exactly what to tell us and how much to let us know.

"Okay, okay," Commander Shaw said, pulling at his long grey beard. "You might want to sit down for this."

Monica and I took seats in the chairs. They were in fact as uncomfortable as they looked.

"Monica and her father have been working with Phoenix long enough that we have had the opportunity to build trust." Commander Shaw eyed me with a heavy sigh. "We haven't had that time, Daniel, but you don't get to where I am without learning how to read people. My gut tells me that I can trust you. That's why you were allowed to keep your weapon, that's why you have free rein in the Vault. So tell me. Am I right? Can I trust you?"

It almost seemed silly. Here he was looking at me asking if he could trust me when he already had. I think he knew the answer. He just wanted to hear it from me.

"Yes," I said. "You can trust me."

He held my gaze a moment longer then nodded.

"Good," the commander said. "What I'm about to tell you now is for your ears only. It's information we have on the fall of Earth, the corporations, and the Order."

Monica's eyes doubled in size. I had to admit in a different life, Commander Shaw could have been a master storyteller. I'd consider myself a pretty hardened individual, but Commander Shaw had me at the edge of my seat.

The story he told us next was impossible. Had I not known what I was or seen the Cyber Hunter for myself, I wouldn't have believed the tale in a million years.

CHAPTER FOUR

"TELL me what you know of the destabilization of Earth," Commander Shaw asked us. "Of when we realized we needed to migrate to the moon and beyond."

"There wasn't enough resources to go around," Monica said with a shrug as if it were information everyone knew. "The Earth was dying and we needed to go find a new home. Not much else to tell."

"That's all correct, but most lies are cloaked in truth. The good ones are at least." Commander Shaw crossed his arms over his chest. "When the governing powers realized what was happening to Earth, they sent their best and brightest to come up with a solution. The Order had them slaughtered."

"The Order didn't want to save Earth?" I asked,

confused. "They wanted to go to the moon? Have they ever been to the moon? It's not that great of a place."

"They had vested interest in history taking a course in which humanity traveled to the moon, Mars, and beyond," Commander Shaw answered. Phoenix was founded in those days humanity abandoned Earth. "We were founded by men and women who knew the very real threats of not the Galactic Government but these shadow entities like the Order and Immortal Corp. The more we pulled on the thread, the more we realized how much they controlled the narrative of mankind."

"And these shadow organizations aren't even on the same side," I chimed in remembering the way Echo tried to convince me to team up against the Cyber Hunter. "They're at each other's throats. The Cyber Hunter was here to kill Echo, maybe even grab the super seed."

"Thanks to you, she got neither," Monica said.

"It was close," I answered, remembering the three-way fight stopped short by the platoon of Phoenix guards rushing into the room. "If we fought it out, I'm not sure who would have been walking out of that cell block."

We stood in silence for the moment as the harsh truth soaked into our minds. I thought back on what

Echo told me about the Order. Another thing struck me.

"Echo said the Order goes as far back as an organization called the Illuminati and the Knights Templar," I said. The tone in my voice asked for clarification on its own. "Do you know what he was talking about?"

"I do," Commander Shaw walked over to the third chair and rested wearily in the seat. He reached into his right pants pocket, pulling out a small vial and downing the substance. "Need to take my medicine these days to dull the edge."

Before I could discern if that was in fact medicine or some kind of alcohol, Commander Shaw dropped another information bomb on us.

"Secret organizations are nothing new. They've been around since the beginning of time. The Order is the oldest known in existence." Commander Shaw placed the empty vial back into his pocket. "Who runs the Order, we don't know. What we do know is that they are real, well-funded, and they've been around as far back as we can determine."

"The Order didn't want humanity to stay on Earth," Monica thought out loud. "They got that. What do they want now? Do they not want Earth terraformed for people to come back?"

"Your guess is as good as mine." Commander Shaw

rose to his feet. He looked exhausted. "I need to report to my superiors. They need to know what's been going on here. But not before we get everything we can out of Echo."

A sour taste came to my mouth. I had no love for Echo. I half wanted to kill him myself, but torture was something different altogether. And it wasn't just that. I knew that Echo wasn't going to give anything up. He'd let himself be tortured over and over again, only to heal and be tortured more.

"Not that," Commander Shaw said, reading my eyes. "Echo isn't going to give us anything willingly. We'll have to go in and extract his memories."

"Extract his memories," Monica repeated. "How?"

"We have a process called cerebral extraction our scientists have been working on," Commander Shaw said, looking over at Monica. "He'll be sedated. We'll send someone into his memories to find out where your father is being held. We're going to get him back."

"I'll go in," Monica said, rising from her chair. "I should be the one to go in. It's my father we need to rescue."

"You're too important to the cause." Commander Shaw shook his head. "We need you. If we can't replicate the super seed effect and manufacture it on a large scale, all of this is for nothing."

"It should be me," I said, rising from my chair. "I have a past with him and my own questions I want answered. I'll go in, get the location of your father, and get my answers while I'm at it."

This seemed to be the outcome Commander Shaw was hoping for. He gave me a tight nod.

"The past can be a brutal place," Monica said, reaching out and touching my arm. "Are you sure you're ready for that?"

"I need to know," I said, looking down at the ground before lifting my eyes to meet hers. "Not knowing is going to eat me alive."

Monica nodded, giving my arm a squeeze before letting her own arm fall to her side. "Be careful."

"I'm going to let the team know to get our room ready," Commander Shaw said, ducking out of the room. "It shouldn't be more than a few minutes."

"Daniel, Monica is right," X said out loud. "Not just because the truth of your past may cause a mental break, but tied so closely to Echo's mind, you might not be able to get out intact."

"What do you mean?" Monica asked, concern etched on her face. "X, what are you talking about?"

"The events Daniel is searching for are so traumatic, if his mind is not able to differentiate reality from Echo's memory, serious harm could occur. This is all hypothetical, of course. Any procedure like this is still in its experimental phase."

"I'm going in," I said with a shrug. "That's it. I'm going in and you're not going to be able to talk me out of it. It's something I have to do."

The tone in my voice was more forceful than I anticipated. X quieted and Monica actually looked angry.

I was saved from having to say anything else as the door in the adjacent room opened. A pair of white-lab-coated scientists walked into the room. They arrived so fast, they had to have been waiting and ready for the green light.

The hover cart they pushed in front of them had a machine full of wires and monitors attached to it. I wasn't even going to pretend I understood how the science worked behind the thing.

Commander Shaw reentered our room. "Are you ready for this, Daniel?"

"Ready," I said, ignoring the glare from Monica. She was a fireball.

I followed the commander out of the viewing room to the holding cell next door. Echo was reclined in a resting position leaning back against his chair instead of the table in front of him.

The scientists placed an IV into his left arm. A chair was brought for me and put on the opposite side of the table from Echo.

I took a seat looking at Echo's disfigured form. The explosion had really torn him apart. The dreadlocks were burned off half his head. His shirt was scorched in a dozen different places. A patch of it near his chest was completely gone.

"Daniel." A short scientist with thick glasses came to me with a ready smile and an open hand. "My name is Doctor Bartelbee. I'll be administering the procedure today. It should be a painless and quick experience."

I accepted his hand and give it a firm but not crushing shake.

"Let's do it," I said.

Our attention was grabbed as the other scientist opened a projector onto the far wall the likes of which I had never seen. Usually projectors were just that. They projected a holographic image on the wall. This one displayed a picture that looked like a wall of monitors. Not the kind of holograms you could see through. They actually looked like six large monitors resting in the wall.

"Technology these days," Doctor Bartelbee said

with an excited laugh. "What will they come up with next, am I right?"

I took the question as rhetorical.

"We'll be able to monitor your progress on the screens," Commander Shaw said. "If things get too much to handle in there, we'll pull you out."

"Just give me enough time to not only get your answers but my own," I said. "Don't pull me out too soon."

"I'll let you stay as long as it's safe for you," Commander Shaw agreed. "You're a good man, Daniel. That's something this galaxy is in short supply of these days. I won't pull you out until you're ready or serious damage could occur."

That was enough for me. I guess it had to be enough at the moment.

"We'll have sedatives running through the IVs attached to both of you, if I may?" Doctor Bartelbee asked, looking down at my arm.

"Go ahead," I said. I leaned back in my chair as something I can only describe as a low-sitting crown was put on my brow from the other scientist. The steel crown felt cold on my forehead as a series of wires connected it to the machine. Another series of wires sprouted out from the machine and to an identical metal piece on Echo's head.

"I have to say I am very excited to see how this will work on men of your—of your origin," Doctor Bartelbee said with an excited grin. "We've only ever tested this on regular humans. I've adjusted the sedative to compensate for your accelerated metabolisms."

The doctor gently pushed the needle of the IV into the vein at the crook of my right elbow. He secured it with a patch of tape before moving on.

"Try and relax," Commander Shaw coached me. "Remember everything you are seeing isn't real right now. They're past memories, nothing more. Focus on where you want Echo's mind to focus. You're driving. He's just the vehicle at this point."

"Got it," I said, already feeling sleepy as the drugs were dumped into my arm. "I control what he thinks about. Piece of cake."

One second I was in the room, the next I was hurtling through what almost looked like space. The entire Vault was gone. All around me was blackness with white lights that shot out from someplace I couldn't see. The lights weren't single dots of light but rather cones that came from some origin point I was headed toward now.

Voices sounded in my ears, too many to distinguish one from the next.

Focus, I reminded myself. *Focus on what you want him*

to remember. You're in control. Focus.

The lights continued to grow in the darkness. The sounds of the voices grew louder and louder until they buzzed inside my head.

Like someone flipped on a light switch and the blackness with the white piercing cone lights was gone. I stood in front of a tall building… on the moon? No, there was no glass structure keeping us safe. We were on Mars, this had to be Mars.

I turned around in wonder. To my recollection, I had never been to Mars before. The place was so vastly different from either Earth or the moon, I was having trouble processing what I was seeing.

Wide-open paved streets allowed people to walk freely. The amount of people within eyesight was also shocking. The moon was packed with people walking shoulder to shoulder to the extent vehicles had to take to the sky. This was not the case on Mars.

On Mars, people strolled by laughing and talking. Vehicles on two, four, and six wheels drove by with more than enough room to spare.

The buildings were spaced far enough apart to have room in between. Intricate sculptures and water fountains peeked out of alleyways and were stationed on the edges of buildings.

A woman walked toward me. I recognized her. X, in

her blue skintight suit and shoulder-length dark hair looked at me, just as surprised to see me as I was to see her. I had only seen her once before in my own dream, when I recalled my past.

"How is this possible?" I asked her. "We're inside Echo's memories and you're here because you were inside mine?"

"We share a special link brought on by the trauma when you were shot in the head," X reminded me. "Anything past that now would be pure speculation on my part."

We stood staring at each other a moment longer. To be honest, I had no idea what to think. X was a part of me now, but if I was honest, I was glad to have her here. Not for the scene that we were about to see in Echo's memories, but for the next.

"There he is." X motioned with her right finger. "He can't see us, but we'll be able to follow him just like when we were in your memory."

I turned to look down the street where X motioned with her hand. Sure enough, Echo was there, and with him, a woman with long red hair. The same woman who was in the half burned picture I recovered from Wesley Cage.

I didn't know who she was yet. But I knew enough to know she was part of the Pack Protocol.

CHAPTER FIVE

I KNEW it was her not just from my memory of the picture, but my own memories of her flashed through my mind like a lightning bolt. Images of the two of us training, sharing meals, and even decked out in full gear for a mission.

I grabbed my temples trying to repress the memories for a later time. As much as I wanted to remember right now I made a promise to Monica to find where her father was being held.

The Mars landscape around me began to blur. Fuzzy blackness threatened to rip away the image in front of me.

"You have to focus, Daniel," X's voice reminded me. "You're in control here. You have to remind Echo's mind that this is where you want him to take you."

Safe house with a laboratory, I forced myself away from the memories of the red headed woman. *Echo where would you take a prisoner that was a safe house but also had the equipment for him to work?*

The skull-spitting pain in my cranium began to subside. The view of Mars around me went from fuzzy back to normal once more.

I stood up, taking a deep, cleansing breath.

"Are you able to continue?" X asked, concerned. "I can probably stop this on my own without the need for them to pull you out."

"No, no not yet. I'm fine," I said, shaking my head free of the pain. I jogged forward to join Echo and the red-headed woman. "Come on. We have to get close enough to hear what they're saying. Any landmarks or city names, street names even, could help us figure out where this is on Mars."

X and I ran across the street to join Echo and his companion as they turned down an alley. Out of the corner of my eye, I saw a statue. It was at least two stories tall. A bronze woman held a sign in her right hand that read "Elysium."

I couldn't ever remember going to Mars, but I knew enough to realize Elysium was one of their most famous cities. At least we knew what city we were in now. All I needed was a street sign or building name to really zero in on the location.

"There," X said with a nod. The alley Echo and the woman walked down sat between two storefronts. One was The Archangel and the other store was called The Elite. "That has to be enough to go on."

"Right, good work," I said, still moving down the alley to follow the pair. "Let's just follow them a bit longer to be sure they're headed to the safe house."

I could tell X didn't like it, but she came along anyway. She was afraid the more of my past I dug up, the harder it would be on me. If I was being honest, I was a little afraid as well.

Stare down a band of Reapers or a Cyber Hunter and count me in. Put me in front of a mirror to my past and I wasn't so sure I could handle it. But I had to.

The alley in Elysium was the cleanest, most pristine alley I had seen in my life. There were expensive high rise apartments on the moon that weren't this clean.

I was close enough now to hear Echo and the woman talking as they made their way to a side door to the right of the alley.

"Really, Samantha?" Echo rolled his eyes. "You know you want to go out with me. You can just admit it. After I saved your life back on that rock, I saw it in you. I was your hero."

"Sorry, I just threw up in my mouth a little," Sam said, pretending to cover her mouth and swallow the vomit back down. "Not going to happen. And I saved you on the viper mission, not the other way around. I think you've had too much brain trauma and it's starting to mess with your head."

"It's just a matter of time." Echo shrugged. "You'll be begging me to go out with you sooner or later. You can't resist the inevitable."

During their conversation, I moved up closer to get a better look at both of them. Echo wasn't much different at all really. The same dreadlocks came down over his long coat. He looked like he was the same age as the Echo I knew now.

Samantha was tall without being thin. Her hair fell behind her in a curtain. I could tell the woman was a poised spring without having to look twice. Her green eyes said it all. She was a killer just like Echo and me. She wore brown boots, dark pants, and a shirt with a short brown jacket.

"Right, well let's get this over with. Any idea what they want this time?" Samantha asked. She entered a key code on the door. I was close enough to see the number: two, two, seven, five, one.

"No idea. I thought we were going to get some downtime back at base." Echo stretched and yawned. A blue light shot out from the key code. Starting from their heads, it scanned them from the top down. "I heard Preacher got some time off after his midnight run."

"Wherever we're off to next, it'll be like all the others," Samantha said with a shrug as the door clicked open. "In and out. They won't know what hit them."

Echo opened the door for Samantha and they walked inside together. I followed close behind along with X.

The building was two stories tall on the outside, unassuming. The inside was the exact opposite. A pair of muscled guards nodded to Echo and Samantha as they headed for a door set into the back of the building.

The guards let them in without question. The way required another biometric scanner, this time for their hands and eye.

This place is going to be a beast to break into, I thought to myself. *There are only two guards here now, but if they know they're protecting the doctor who is going to create the super seed for them, there will be a lot more when we come.*

We walked down a steep flight of steps that led to

an underground level full of glass walls and workers. I couldn't see what the scientists were creating, but they were busy.

Echo and Samantha ignored the level for the most part. They took a hard right down a long corridor that ended with another door. This door didn't have a lock. They stepped inside a circular room with three screens mounted on the far wall.

As soon as we entered the room, the screens clicked to life, showing the shadow figures of three individuals sitting in high-backed chairs. The light was perfect, so we couldn't see their faces at all, only their silhouettes. Two were men, one was a woman, at least as far as the outlines could tell me.

"You two have done well," the woman in the center screen said, beginning the conversation. "I know we're usually able to give you a bit more of a break between runs, but there's a matter that needs immediate attention."

The room quieted. Echo and Samantha remained still, not quite at attention but making sure it was clear they were respectful and all ears.

"The matter at hand is sensitive," the man on the left screen said in a deep, rumbling voice. "You two were hand-selected for this task because we believe the two of you understand the core mission of Immortal Corp more so than any other operatives. You understand sacrifices will have to be made and hard orders carried out."

"There's no easy way to say this, so I'm just going to come out with it." The woman reined in the conversation. "One of our own needs to be put down. She refuses to listen to orders, and she's a liability not only to herself but to the entire company now. I think you know who it is."

"Amber," Echo breathed.

When I heard the name, I felt half sick, half angered. I came here thinking I was going to find out where Monica's father was being held, not that my own answers would be part of the same memory.

My hands clenched into fists.

"I'm sure you two have sensed a change in her recently." The man with the gravel voice was back. "She's lost sight of our mission. She's lost sight of who she is. If given enough time, we're afraid she'll turn against us and maybe even turn others against us as well."

I moved to the side of the room where I could see Echo and Samantha's facial expressions as well as the dark figures in the monitors. I wasn't sure what I expected to see.

Echo and Samantha wore similar looks on their faces. Confusion and sadness rested in their eyes.

"What we do shapes the future and allows humanity to prepare for the coming threats we will face together. And make no mistake, the threats will come," the woman said in a hard tone. "We cannot allow one of ours to be derailed. You two are to neutralize number three immediately."

A silence fell over the room so palpable, I swear I felt a heaviness on my shoulders.

"Number four, number five, is there a problem with your orders?" the woman asked. "Speak now. We understand she's a member of the Pack. Turning on one of your own isn't what we do here, but the circumstance has become dire."

"Perhaps she would see reason if I spoke to her?" Samantha asked hesitantly. "I understand what must be done, but maybe if there's even a chance I could get through to her—"

"She's made her choice," the man with the deep voice boomed. "She's tried to make contact with the Order."

"Oh, Amber, no," Samantha breathed.

"So that you understand there is no going back for her, I want to play a transmission we intercepted," the woman said, reaching a four-fingered right hand to a recording device on the desk in front of her. "This is all the proof you'll need."

"The killing needs to stop on both our sides," a young woman's voice filled the room.

Tears sprang to my eyes as if on command. I recognized that voice. How could I have ever forgotten it? It was Amber.

"I'm done being a puppet for Immortal Corp. If even a small part of you feels the same way about the Order, we can build on that. If you are receiving this, you can trust me. There has to be a different way than assassination missions on the populace as a whole and one another," Amber spoke with excitement as if she were giving an inspirational speech at some kind of celebration. "There are good people on both sides of this. I know one. I'm in love with one. He'll come around. More people will come around. We just have to have the courage and take a stand to be the first."

The transmission ended.

"You know who she's talking about," the woman said. "She's going to try and turn Daniel against the rest of the pack and then she'll manipulate you one by one. Amber, number three, needs to be silenced immediately."

CHAPTER SIX

FOR THE SECOND TIME, the room quieted.

"I don't have to remind you what would happen to you if either of you were to make a lapse in judgment and say, let number three go or fail to take care of her," the man with the booming voice said. "Are we clear on that point?"

"Yes," Echo said, swallowing hard.

Samantha remained quiet.

"Samantha? Number four, do you understand what we're saying to you?" the woman asked. "Are we clear?"

"Yes, ma'am, it's clear," Samantha said, standing straighter, if that were even possible. "I understand what I have to do."

"Good. We'll be operating outside of normal parameters on this one," the woman said with finality in her voice. "There is no need to check in with Cage. He will be informed of what is going on at a later time. You both are to take care of number three immediately. You are to make contact once it is done."

The woman's screen clicked off, as did the man's with the deep voice. The third and last screen remained on for a second longer. This man, at least I guessed it was a man by his outline, hadn't spoken once.

Echo and Samantha looked at him as if he were going to say something.

I even thought he was going to speak. He leaned forward in his chair. As if rethinking his actions, he sat back and his screen also clicked off.

"I can't believe—"

"I don't want to talk about it," Samantha said, storming out of the room and cutting off Echo. "I need a minute."

We stood there together, Echo, X, and I watching Samantha go.

Echo hung his head. His immediate action was anger. He pounded the wall with a fist, breaking through the thin wood on the second punch. He slumped on the ground, blood oozing from the broken skin over his knuckles.

Echo sat there swallowing hard. He wasn't crying, but I could see the level of rage that lived in his eyes.

"Why, why did you have to do this?" Echo asked to no one. "Why, why?"

X and I hadn't spoken to each other since we entered the safe house.

"You have the information you need for the location of the safe house and what happened to Amber. I know you feel like you have to see it, but you don't, Daniel. You don't have to do this to yourself," X said softly. "You don't have to put yourself through this."

"If I don't, then maybe she died for nothing," I said, trying to figure out exactly how I felt on the matter. "I'm not going to let that happen. Someone has to remember. Someone has to talk about it."

Echo, think back to when you killed Amber, I thought to myself, concentrating on the order. *Think of when you and Samantha killed her.*

The room swirled and changed around us. It shifted to black with those cones of white light and a thousand voices talking at once.

The next thing I knew, we were standing on a rooftop overlooking some kind of manmade lake on Mars. On either side of us, rooftops sprawled out. In front of us, the still water lapped the sandy shore. It was midday and bright. There were a handful of locals walking and laughing while others drove by on their vehicles, listening to music or the latest entertainment show on their speakers.

X and I stood just behind Echo and Samantha. Both of them were dressed in black from head to toe. They looked out over the water to a series of buildings on the other side of the lake.

"I'm not doing this," Samantha said, not bothering to turn and look at Echo. "I'm not going to do this."

"Sam, they'll kill us if we don't," Echo said with a low, sad tone. "You know that as well as I do. Maybe not today. Maybe not tomorrow, but they'll eventually find us and kill us."

"If I do this, I'm already dead," Sam said, turning to Echo. "At least the part of me that matters the most will be."

When she turned, I got a better look at her profile. Her hair was tied back in a ponytail now. She wore dark glasses over her eyes. Although she wore a coat, I could tell a blaster rested on her left hip.

"You don't think I want to do this?" Echo gritted his teeth, also turning to her. "The Pack is the only family any of us ever had. Whatever you think about Immortal Corp, they gave us purpose. They gave us a life and a family. If we don't do this, all of that gets ripped apart."

"We're already being ripped apart," Sam said, shaking her head. "And you're right. We are a family. Amber is like a sister to me. I'm not going to kill my sister because she believes differently than I do."

"She doesn't just believe differently than we do." Echo shook his head so violently, the dreadlocks on his head whipped from side to side. "She wants to start an insurrection. She was trying to communicate with the enemy."

"I'm not doing it," Sam said, taking a step back from Echo. Her hand traveled to the blaster at her hip. "I'm not. I'm not going to try to kill you any more than I'm going to try and kill Amber. But I can't control your actions. If you want to try and stop me from leaving, you can try now."

I didn't know what to think. I was so sure that Amber had been betrayed by both Echo and Sam. The deep, hollow feeling in my gut brought on by anger and sadness was still there, but something lived along with it now. It felt like pride, a tiny light of hope shone amidst the maelstrom of heartache.

Echo took a step back, creating distance between himself and Samantha. He slowly let his right hand descend to his belt. Tears fell down his face.

"I have to kill her because that was what I was ordered to do," Echo said, swallowing hard. "I wasn't ordered to kill you. But I might be one day and I'll have to. You're turning your back on the Pack now, not just me."

"Immortal Corp created us, but they don't get to choose who we become," Sam said, turning her back on Echo. She moved to the edge of the rooftop. "If you want to come after me one day, I'll understand. I won't be hard to find. I heard Earth's nice this time of year."

"Don't." Echo shook his head. "I don't want to know where you're going if I'm ever ordered to find you one day."

"Good bye, Echo," Sam said with one last look.

Echo dried his eyes. The muscle in his jaw twitched with anger as he mentally prepared himself for what came next.

Sam jumped off the building edge to a balcony below and made her way to the street. A minute later, she disappeared into the neighborhood.

I stood stunned. I still wasn't sure what to think. I hated Echo and I think a part of me would always hate him. There was still something about seeing the frustration and tears in his own eyes. He had killed Amber and I was going to put him in his grave for that, but he had not been eager or willing to carry out the execution.

How did you kill her, Echo, I forced myself to think. *How did you do it?*

I fast forwarded through Echo's memory. I knew I couldn't watch it in real time. I had to see it to confirm her death, but I had no desire for it to play out second by agonizing second in front of me.

Echo positioned himself on a bridge over the lake. Amber drove by in a small vehicle made for one person. There was a fat tire in the front and another on the rear.

She was gorgeous, her honey-blonde hair, those kind yet fierce eyes. I was reminded of it all right before she died.

Echo hid behind a light pole until the last minute. Just as her small vehicle passed Echo pivoted from behind the light pole, tossing a circular metal explosive onto the side of Amber's transportation. The explosive stuck on to the metal beeped a moment later and exploded.

Amber had a second to realize what was going on but no time to react.

I stood on the sidewalk, shaking half in rage half in grief.

There's nothing you can do, I had to remind myself over and over again. *This all already happened. There's nothing you can do.*

X stood with me, her hand on my shoulder.

Amber's vehicle blew apart into a dozen different sections. She was thrown ten meters to the opposite side of the bridge. Civilians screamed and turned their own vehicles in the opposite direction.

Echo walked over to where a bloody Amber lay in the sidewalk. Despite the damage her body took, she was already struggling to her feet. Crimson red pooled around her. Her left arm looked useless, a mess of bone and flesh.

She screamed in pain then reached for something at her waist.

Echo laid into her with a short-barrel heavy blaster.

I wiped the tears from my eyes as I saw her take round after round from his weapon. The warrior spirit in her couldn't quit, and for that, a smile cracked my lips despite a lump the size of my fist in my throat.

Amber was a fighter until the end. She had reached to her hip to grab a knife. Echo stalked toward her, emptying his clip into her battered body. As soon as he was close enough, Amber struck at him with a roar on her bloody lips. She sank the blade deep into the left side of his neck.

Echo screamed in pain. He reached for a syringe in his own pocket, taking it out and ramming it in Amber's neck. He pressed down on the plunger.

There were sirens in the distance now. Praetorians in their heavy armored trucks were making their way onto the opposite side of the bridge. It didn't seem like the GG messed around on Mars. The attack couldn't have taken more than a few minutes and already first responders were on the scene.

Amber's eyes rolled into the back of her head as Echo pulled the needle free. She slumped in his arms.

Echo ripped her blade free from his neck with a grunt.

"Don't—don't hurt him," Amber said, trying to recover from the drugs in her system. "He doesn't know. He wasn't—a part of this."

"I know," Echo said, reaching into his opposite jacket pocket for a long wire. He attached one end to her leg and the other he secured around the rail of the bridge that was made from some kind of white stone.

Echo reloaded his weapon then blasted a section of the rock next to the anchored end Amber wore around her leg. He fired his weapon a second time at the section of the bridge railing on the other side of Amber's anchor. All the decimated rock railing would need now was a hard shove to fall over the edge of the bridge.

"You don't have to be who they created you to be," Amber said, struggling to get up, still half out of her mind with the drugs introduced into her system. "You don't have to let your past define who you are today."

Echo picked her up gently as if he were carrying some child he genuinely cared about.

"I'm sorry," Echo said to her. "This is what I am."

I couldn't help it. I was losing my hold on the moment. I knew it was a memory that I had no control over. Still, everything in my being demanded I act.

"No!" I screamed, racing forward and trying to grasp at Amber's body as she was dropped into the lake below.

My hand reached for hers, only going through it instead of being able to actually hold it. The strangest thing was Amber's face looked content. Not an expression of fear as I would imagine in someone's last minute when they realized they were about to be drowned. She looked as if she were at peace with her end.

Amber's body hit the water, ripping the rock piece off the bridge after her with the aid of another blast from Echo's weapon.

The rock slammed into the river after her. Echo raced off as the GG praetorians arrived on the scene.

I didn't really care about seeing Echo escape or about following the actions of the GG praetorians around me. I fell to my knees, staring at the rippling water that marked Amber's grave.

I felt sick to my stomach, and my head hurt once again like someone was driving a pickaxe through the back of my skull. An impossible desperation overtook me that maybe, just maybe Amber was going to somehow rise to the surface.

Maybe she had managed to get away by some miracle. I shook so hard I couldn't stop myself. Tears came and fell down my face unabated.

X knelt next to me. I could see her out of my peripheral vision, but I wasn't really in the mood to have a conversation.

Neither was X. She placed her hand on top of mine and gave me a squeeze, not saying anything.

The maelstrom of emotion built inside of me. Grief turned to anger. I lifted my head to the sky. A scream ripped from my throat that started as anguish but somewhere halfway through ended in rage.

Wake up! I screamed at Echo in my head. *Wake up! I'm going to kill you.*

CHAPTER SEVEN

I CAME out of my drugged state in pure adrenaline mode. One second I was in Echo's memory of Amber's death. The next I was sitting across from him surrounded by Phoenix guards and lab-coated scientists.

My eyes blinked open at the same time Echo's did. I had no idea if he realized I was in his head or not. I didn't care. I was going to kill him.

Commander Shaw saw the look in my eyes even before I ripped the IV out of my arm and leapt over the table.

"Daniel, don't," Commander Shaw said, reaching for my arm.

He was too slow. The metal crown I wore that

connected me to Echo's dream state was jerked off my head as I vaulted over the table, slamming into Echo.

Echo was chained to his chair and took the brunt of my tackle full on. His chair tipped over, tearing the IV out and the crown off his head as well.

"You didn't have to do it!" I screamed at him. My hands found his neck. "Sam didn't do it. You didn't have to do it!"

Echo's eyes bulged out of his skull. His latest injuries left a face looking at me half-scarred from the damage, half-white skull as tendons and ligaments healed over.

"Daniel!" Monica burst into the room. "Stop! You have to stop!"

Hands reached for my shoulders and arms, trying to pry me off.

"He can tell us more," Commander Shaw said as he and other guards wrestled my arms free. "Daniel, we need him alive."

I was past all reason. My hands trembled as I choked the life out of Echo. Echo couldn't get a word out, since I was strangling him, but he didn't try to break free. He looked me dead in my eyes and gave the slightest nod as if he were giving me permission to kill him.

"What did she die for, Daniel?" X asked softly in my head. Although her voice was the quietest compared to the shouting around me, it cut through my fog of rage like a steel wire through butter. "Echo has information that can help her cause. The future she saw."

I wasn't really counting, but I must have had three or four Phoenix guards trying to pry me off Echo's throat at the moment.

I could have killed him there. Maybe I should have. Left to my own devices, I knew I would. X was right. Echo had a wealth of information we could access in his memory bank, all of which would help us not only free Monica's father but unlock answers to my past and help us bring down Immortal Corp for good.

Reluctantly, I let go of Echo's throat.

Echo gasped for air, choking on the lungsful of oxygen coming back into his body.

"Kill me!" Echo coughed. "No, you have to kill me. What are you doing?"

I sat back on my heels. I gave the guards who still held me looks that spoke murder for them if they didn't let me go. They got the hint. As one, they released me.

I stood up, looking down at Echo's prone form.

The room quieted. Everyone waited to see what I would do next.

"I deserve to die," Echo said as spittle flew from his mouth. He coughed again. "You saw what I did. I killed her. I deserve to die. Kill me!"

"No," I said, turning for the door. "It's not what she would have wanted. You may have killed her, but you didn't kill her spirit or the future she saw. That lives on."

I left the room, chased by the roars of madness coming out of Echo's tortured soul.

Monica caught up with me outside the hall of the room.

"Daniel, wait," Monica said, running in front of me to stop my forward progress. "We saw everything you did thanks to those monitors that tracked your progress. Thank you, thank you for finding out where my father is. I'm so—so sorry for what you had to see. I wish there was something I could do. Amber was an amazing woman with a wonderful heart and vision for the future."

I nodded. I kind of felt numb at the moment. After the pain and fury left, I felt like I could eat a dropship and sleep for a week.

Memories of where Sam said she was going kept my physical needs at bay.

"I'm going to help you get your father back," I told Monica. "That hasn't changed. But I have to make a trip first."

"We won't be ready to go to Mars for another day or two," Commander Shaw said, joining us in the hall. "I have to report all of this. We'll need to get identities for you to get in and out of Mars. The Galactic Government has the planet buttoned up tight."

"Every day we wait puts my father's life in jeopardy," Monica said, trying to restrain the stress in her tone. "We have to go as soon as possible."

"And we will," Commander Shaw reassured her. "But we're not going to do your father any good if we can't get onto the planet, or once there, you're recognized and taken into custody. We can bet that Immortal Corp has labeled both of you as traitors and uploaded your information to the Galactic Government database. They'll use the GG to bring you in then extract you from them."

"Two days?" I asked.

"That's a safe bet," Commander Shaw said with a tight nod. He read something in my question. "Why?"

"How far away are the Badlands?" I asked, remembering Sam told Echo she was coming to Earth. That and the story of the red-haired woman I heard in the diner outside of New Vegas, it had to be her. "They're to the north?"

"By air, you can be there in a few hours, but I can't give you access to a dropship, Daniel," Commander Shaw said. "I mean, as an outsider not affiliated with Phoenix, it would be impossible to get you clearance. Now if we could schedule a routine pass over the Badlands and you just happened to stow aboard and, say, drop out of the rear hatch, well, I don't think we could stop you."

I went from trying to figure out how I was going to get to the Badlands to grinning a second later. "Thank you."

"Don't thank me. I didn't do anything." Commander Shaw turned to walk back down the hall. "If there were going to be a dropship making that routine pass, it would be leaving within the hour."

Monica watched as Commander Shaw left the hall.

"He's a good man," Monica said. "I get why you have to go. It sounds selfish if I only think about myself and my father. I understand if you can't make it back in time when we leave for Mars."

"Two days," I told her. "I gave you my word. I'll be back in two days. Wait for me. Commander Shaw said it would take that long to make arrangements anyway."

Monica gave me a tight nod. Her eyes lit up a second later.

"I almost forgot. I have something for you." Monica waved me into the viewing room adjacent to the one I had just been in.

When we walked inside, we were just in time to see four Phoenix guards walk out with a heavily chained Echo. Doctor Bartelbee and his assistant were still gathering their equipment.

"He'll need more of the serum if his body is going to be able to maintain what was done to it," Doctor Bartelbee was instructing his counterpart. "He'll eventually need to go into the sleep again. I can't imagine what he must feel like. I mean, to be asleep for so many years and then wake up only when there's conflict. What a life."

Monica and I looked at one another, confused. It was clear the two scientists had no idea we were in the opposite room and able to listen in. I wasn't really a nosy person by default, but the topic they were speaking on was far too interesting not to.

"How old do you think he really is?" the assistant asked. He was much younger than Doctor Bartelbee with long slicked-back hair and a slight lisp. "I've heard stories that he was alive when the Earth fell. But they're just stories."

"I wouldn't doubt them in the slightest. It might be better that we don't know too much," Doctor Bartelbee said, pushing the hover cart through the door. "Anyway, want to grab dinner soon? I'm in the mood for anything at the moment besides Mexican. I had that last night and let me tell you, my last visit to the bathroom looked like a murder scene."

Monica and I looked to each other with first a grimace and then a chuckle.

"Who do you think they were talking about?" Monica asked, going over to the single table in the room where a dark grey case sat. It wasn't there the first time I entered the chamber.

"I don't know," I said, shaking my head free of images of Doctor Bartelbee stuffing his face with Mexican food. "What's in the case?"

"When we got here, I put in a rush request with our armor team," Monica said, opening the case in front of me. "I told them to get it to me as soon as it was finished."

I looked down at the open case, not sure what I was seeing. It looked like a clip for my MK II but ended in a small drum the size of my fist.

"I know you had to swap out which type of ammunition to use by removing and putting different packs into the hand cannon," Monica explained. "The drum holds all four types of rounds now: gas, explosive, knockout rounds, and normal. Instead of having to swap out charge packs, they're all in one. The drum allows for you to be able to hold forty rounds all together."

I picked up the drum, reaching to my lower back with my free hand to draw my weapon. I released the current charge pack and clipped in the drum. It fit perfectly. The end of the handle was a bit bulky now with the drum, but it wouldn't inhibit my ability to draw the weapon. I might have to mount it on my hip now, but that would be worth the trade off if it did what Monica said.

"Thank you," I said, testing the weight and feel over and over again.

"That's not even the best part," Monica said, practically beaming with pride. "There's a pressure-sensitive smart reader mounted on the upper section of the pack. Now when your designated fingerprint applies pressure to different areas of the weapon it tells the drum which rounds to fire."

I looked down at the MK II with newfound respect.

"If you move your thumb up and press, it's your normal steel rounds. Slightly down, you have your knockout rounds. Below that is gas and finally explosive rounds," Monica explained. As she listed off the rounds in the barrel, she pointed to the section on the side of the MK II near my thumb. "Try it. You'll feel a slight rotation as the barrel maneuvers your desired rounds in place."

I moved my thumb as far down the grip as I could while still holding it with one hand and pressed. True to Monica's words, I felt a slight movement within the drum on the weapon as the desired rounds were shifted into place. I did the same pressing the gas rounds and then the knockout rounds and finally my traditional steel bolts. Every time I pressed, the smart drum read my thumb pressure and maneuvered the rounds in place.

"This is great," I said, looking up at Monica. "Thank you. I have a feeling I'm going to need this in the coming days."

"Just be safe out there," Monica said, taking a step closer. She leaned in and gave me a kiss on the cheek.

Her soft lips pressed against the hard stubble on the left side of my face.

How long has it been since you've been kissed by a woman? I asked myself with no answer. *Was Amber the last?*

I wasn't sure if Monica wanted more or if it was a simple gesture for a hurting friend. I guess it didn't really matter. I didn't have more to give her at the moment.

"Thank you," I said over my shoulder as I turned. "I'll be back in two days. We'll get your father. I promise."

CHAPTER EIGHT

MY STOMACH WAS PRACTICALLY EATING itself by the time I reached the hangar bay. The events of the morning had been like trying to hold on to some runaway dropship. I didn't know what time it was now, but I was pretty sure I had missed at least one meal, maybe two.

The energy my body used to heal me from the fight with the Cyber Hunter needed to be replenished and fast.

I saw the four dropships in line as maintenance crews went over checks. One of the ships on the end had its rear cargo bay door down. I jogged over to the ramp, stopping by a supply rack on my right to find an appropriate harness for my new weapon.

The MK II I usually placed on the small of my back

wouldn't fit there comfortably anymore thanks to the drum pack. I settled for a harness that would strap the weapon, not to my waist, but rather to the thigh on the outside of my right leg.

The MK II would be within perfect grabbing distance stationed right where my hand naturally hung from my arm.

I wasn't one for armor, but I saw the value in wearing it now. I had no idea what I was in store for, traveling into the Badlands to the north.

I chose a lightweight armor suit that would protect me from everything except high caliber weapons. It almost felt silly placing the pieces of armor around my body. I'd heal from everything short of someone drowning me as far as I knew. Still it would be better not to have to deal with the pain of a blade or round if I didn't have to.

"Yo, we going to pretend you're not on this ship while I make my rounds or what?" a voice much too young to be in the Phoenix base at all called out. "I got a schedule to keep here."

I looked up from clipping on my chest protection. A short man barely out of his teens stood on the open rear ramp of the dropship. He rested his hand on his waist, not trying to hide the idea that I was inconveniencing him.

He wore a one-piece jumpsuit that was dark tan. The fiery look in his bright eyes matched the Phoenix emblem on his right shoulder. Above the pocket on the left side of his chest was the designation "331TRS."

"I'm coming," I said, jogging across the hangar bay. My stomach rumbled so loud, I thought for sure it would cause an echo in the colossal room. "So I don't have to sneak aboard or anything? You'll just let me on?"

"I don't know nothing, and I want to keep it that way," the young man said, extending a hand. "Name's Riner."

"Good to meet you," I said, taking his hand and following him onboard. "Thanks for the lift."

"No idea what you're talking about," Riner said with a shrug.

We walked past the open cargo bay area in the rear of the dropship and made our way through the seating section that remained empty and to the pilot's cabin.

A woman as old as Riner was young looked back at me with a raised eyebrow. A mischievous light twinkled in her eye.

"You him?" she asked in a thick accent I didn't recognize. She wore the same uniform and insignia as Riner. "No offense, I thought you'd be taller. I mean, the way everyone is talking about how you took on a

Cyber Hunter and such nonsense. I thought they was a myth and all. My lord, this day and age, who knows what's fact or fiction anymore."

I was about to open my mouth to respond when the woman continued.

"You look hungry," she said with a motherly scowl. "Raised three boys of my own so I recognize that look well enough."

She waved to a third seat behind the pilot's and co-pilot's chairs. A small compartment under the seat caught my attention.

"I store snacks and such for when the time calls," she said, turning back to her control panel. "You're welcome to them now."

"Thank you," I said, feeling a sense of relief that I would actually be able to eat. "I didn't get your name."

"Lori," the older woman said, turning to her control panel. She fastened her seatbelt and went over the pre-flight check like the true professional she was.

"Mustang Lori," Riner said in the seat next to her with a grin.

"Mustang?" I asked, taking my seat behind the two. I opened the compartment below my feet and reached inside. I was rewarded with a canteen of water, dried meat, some kind of cheese in a can, and crackers.

"Just a nickname I picked up over the years. Now

my dropship goes by the same name," Lori called back to me. "You best strap in tight, Immortal Man. We're fixing to take off right about now."

"Yes, ma'am," I said around a mouthful of cheese. Her nickname for me brought a smile.

I secured the harness that came over my head in a V shape. It secured to a buckle that rose from the seat between my legs.

"This is Vault to Mustang," a voice crackled over the radio. "Mustang, we're opening the hangar bay doors now."

"Roger, Vault," Lori said into the headset she placed over her short haircut. "Initiating pre-flight check followed by thrusters."

"Good to go," Riner said in his co-pilot seat as he too placed a headset over his ears. "Thrusters in two, one, ignition."

I felt the dropship rumble to life below me. I was as happy as a kid in a candy store at the moment. I shoved a handful of the crackers into my mouth that were more salt than anything else but tasted just fine to me. There wasn't a large variety of the snack foods, but there was a lot of it.

I looked around Lori's seat to see the gigantic hangar bay doors begin to slide open. The steel pieces had to be ten, maybe twelve stories tall. They moved slowly, letting in the warm afternoon sun. The rays touched my face like someone's soothing fingers against my cold skin.

"Here we go," Lori said over the sound of the engines. "Hold on to your snacks."

The dropship kicked off the ground and shot forward with a holler and whoop from Riner. This was nothing like the other dropship ride I had taken from the moon to Earth.

The feeling of being sick touched my stomach. I had to close my eyes and steady myself before opening them again. The dropship raced through the sky. I was immediately impressed by the idea that the Vault was located in a mountain range. As such, the hangar bay doors opened on the side of the mountain. In front of us was more of the mountain range, to the left the dead sea, and the right, more desert.

I focused on chewing and filling the emptiness in my stomach rather than concentrating on how fast we must be traveling. On the up side, I didn't experience the same feeling of sickness as my previous trip in a dropship. Maybe I was getting used to it.

You got it, keep it together, I told myself. *You can go head to head with a Cyber Hunter, but you can't go for a little joy ride?*

"Traveling this fast, we're going to be there in no

time," Lori shouted behind her. "Anywhere specific that we'd be headed in the Badlands?"

I racked my brain, trying to remember the name of the city the woman at the diner had mentioned. Although she hadn't spoken English, she had recognized my tattoo and her translator spoke for her.

These thoughts led me to the guilt of both women's death. I was reminded that her translator wasn't just another person. It had been a relative to her, maybe a granddaughter or grandniece. I wasn't sure if their blood was on my hands, but I felt that guilt sit in my belly like the dried meat I gorged myself with.

"X," I asked under the sounds of the engines. "You remember the name of the city in the Badlands?"

"The name of the city they referenced was called Cecile. Daniel, we need to talk," X said in a worried voice. "The trauma of the memories you witnessed, of Amber dying, can't be bottled up and moved past this quickly. You need time to process and talk to someone about it. If not me, then someone else."

"Thanks, I'm good," I lied.

I knew X was probably right, but right now, I had one thing on my mind and that was finding Sam in the Badlands. Finding her led to even more answers and answers were the only thing I had on my mind at the moment.

"You know of a town in the Badlands called Cecile?" I leaned forward and shouted at the back of Lori's seat.

Lori didn't turn around and look at me, but Riner sure did. His eyes were huge. He looked at me like I had just grown a second head or confessed that I was actually a Cyber Hunter.

"Why do you want to go to Cecile?" Lori asked. The normal joyful almost playful kick in the woman's voice was gone. In its place was something like cautious dread.

"It's where I'm going to find the answers I need," I responded, just as guarded. "Why? What's in Cecile?"

Both Lori and Riner sat quiet. Neither of them made a sound for a long minute.

"We can drop him off without having to land," Riner said to Lori. "That was the plan anyway. He can chute in."

Lori remained quiet.

I wished I could have seen the expression on her face, try to read her somehow to get a gauge on what was going on here. Whatever the case, these two were not hot on the idea of heading to the city in the Badlands.

down the barrel of his long rifle. "So where does that leave us now?"

"If you won't show me the shoulder, then I'm going to have to take that as you do have a wolf tattoo there." The bartender licked his fat, greasy lips. "And if that's the case, we'll put you down and chain you. Those were her orders."

I played the events about to transpire over in my mind. I saw myself in my mind's eye disarm the bartender, leap over the counter, and open fire on the crowded room.

"Before we do this," I asked over my shoulder. "Does anyone want to leave?"

No answer. The still in the room was so heavy, it fell on our shoulders like a real weight.

I swatted the bartender's rifle out of the way a second before it went off. I vaulted over the counter as the first blaster rounds scorched the bar around me. The massive shelf full of alcohol bottles behind the bar erupted in a shower of glass and liquid as rounds missed me and detonated.

I fell to relative safety on the other side of the bar on top of the bartender. He looked at me with an open mouth, trying to free his rifle.

I slammed my right fist into his jaw, sending him into unconsciousness as I relieved him of his rifle and drew the MK II from its holster. I pressed my thumb into the section of the weapon that called for explosive rounds. The drum at the base of the weapon rumbled and obeyed, sending the explosive rounds to the forefront of the charge pack.

I sat there with my back against the inside of the bar as rounds struck my hiding spot. All around, they discharged on the wood of the bar and the glass shelving above. Glass and liquor rained down on my head like some kind of confetti.

"Did every single one of them have a weapon?" X asked inside my head. "Holy bananas."

"Holy bananas is right," I said as those firing the rounds took a break.

More than hundred rounds had to have been fired from the time I leapt over the bar and took cover. My hair was drenched in horrible smelling liquid, as were my armor and weapons. That pissed me off.

"You think you can call out targets for me that have the highest powered weapons?" I asked. "Anyone with a heavy repeater or scatter gun should go first."

"I'll call out the shots," X said. "But if you're here to try and talk to Sam and not fight, it might be best to minimize the body count. If you can."

"They're trying to kill us," I reminded X.

"Right, because they think you're going to kill Sam," X reminded me. "Just a thought."

"I'll see what I can do. I'm not much for a countdown," I told her. "Ready?"

"Let's do it," X answered.

X was amazing. More than amazing, she was laser-fast in picking my targets.

I rose from behind the bar, already running sideways to my left. I held my MK II in my right hand with the explosive rounds and the heavy rifle in my left. As soon as I was up, I noticed two things. Everyone in the room did in fact have some kind of weapon and they were pointing it at me.

For the second time, the room erupted in a hail of weapons fire.

Using my own vision, X laced my targets one by one with a red diamond on their person. First she marked a big guy by the door holding a pair of heavy repeaters.

Instead of aiming at his body, I planted an explosive round at his feet. It shouldn't kill him but was guaranteed to take him out of the fight.

When I took him out, she targeted a woman close by with a wide-barreled rifle, and so on and on we went.

Even though I kept moving and the explosive

rounds were taking out numerous targets at once without killing them, there was no escaping the maelstrom of fire. I was a magnet for the stuff and it was bound to happen.

A round hit me in the chest. The light Phoenix armor I wore was enough to turn the blow. Another hit me in my shoulder. That one hurt. Fiery pain exploded across my body.

The whole time, I was running sideways behind the bar. My lane was about to be cut short. The bar ended in a chest-high wall.

I turned the MK II, blasting a smoking hole in the wall, and kept going. I didn't really have a plan besides attack.

I went after them head on, rushing into the weapons fire. A feeling of animalistic rage filled my heart. It was terrifying and comfortable all at once. Another round hit me in the leg, causing me to stumble. I rolled across the floor, keeping my feet under me, and popped up at a run again.

Another round hit the rifle I held, ripping it from my hand. Another tear of agony tore through my left palm.

It was all over for them now. I was among them. Their superior numbers meant nothing. It was hand-to-hand combat, and unless they wanted to chance hitting one of their own, their superior fire power meant nothing.

I moved like water, fluid, from one assailant to the next. A strike to the throat led to me placing a pair of rounds into the legs of two more targets, led to ducking a blow from a fourth and planting the crown of my head squarely into his nose, sending him to the floor.

I did what I was created to do and I loved it. There was a part of me lost in the rage of war that was terrified. Somewhere, I knew in the back of my mind, I shouldn't enjoy or relish the adrenaline pumping through my veins or the fact that my vision turned a hint of red when I fought.

Once I ate through half of their number, they started to panic. Some fled screaming for help while others too frightened to do anything else but discharge their weapon fired on their own.

That was what I anticipated. I moved quickly from target to target. Those who chose to attack me I dealt with quickly and efficiently. Those who still chose to fire their weapon only landed rounds into members on their own side. I used each individual I battled as a shield as much as a punching bag.

I almost felt sorry for them, almost.

When the last enemy fell, I was alone in the room.

My MK II smoked, sending white tendrils to the ceiling. My chest heaved as I looked around at the chaos around me.

You didn't have a choice, I told the part of my mind that said I could have saved some of them. Although I hadn't been the one directly responsible for killing any of them, enough bodies lay bent and broken around me to know long recovery times lay in store for most of them. *You did what you had to do. They were going to kill you or at least try.*

I didn't see the arrow that impaled itself in the left side of my neck, but I sure felt it.

A sour tang filled my throat as I fell to my knees. Suddenly, my legs were no longer able to support my weight. I pulled the arrow free, looking at the tip. The end was fitted with some kind of small syringe.

My arms fell at the same time my face hit the floor.

X was yelling something in my head, but I was past understanding any words.

The last thing I saw was a pair of boots walking toward me. One of them lifted and came down like a hammer on my face.

CHAPTER THIRTEEN

I WOKE with that same sour tang in the back of my throat. I turned my head to the side, trying to spit the taste out. Memories from some delusional dream I had caressed my mind. Despite the causes of the onset of the dream, the dream itself had been comforting.

Something about Amber, the way she kissed me. She told me it was all right, talked to me about a dream that put all other dreams to shame.

That was all gone now as I took in my surroundings. I was chained. Manacles cut into my wrists. Thick chains connected the cuffs to the ceiling. I fought the pounding in my head as I moved to a standing position, taking the weight off my wrists. My armor was gone, as were my weapons. My wounds had already healed.

"X?" I croaked. "X, you there?"

"I am," X said. "How's the head?"

"Feels like it got crushed with a two by four," I said, looking around the small room. It was nothing to write home about. Stone walls with a single door fastened shut. A small window with four bars sat behind me high up in the uppermost section of a ten-foot wall.

"I see through your eyes and they were closed once you were knocked out, but I did have my external speakers active," X explained. "We were moved to a building not far away from the bar where we were ambushed. I heard a woman doling out orders to search then chain you. She instructed them to take you here until she gave further orders. She also stationed a dozen guards outside the door with orders to shoot if you came out."

"A dozen?" I asked. "You think—you think it's Sam? It has to be, right?"

"It's possible, at least all roads lead in that direction," X said. "With the order she gave the bartender and everyone in the bar, it seems she's been expecting a visit from someone from the Pack."

I remembered the bartender and his insistence on seeing my tattoo. X was right. Sam had anticipated Immortal Corp coming after her. She figured they'd send one of her own after her just like they did to Amber.

Except she got it wrong. I had no desire to harm her. I just wanted answers. Maybe even to thank her for not going along with Echo. Was that how I really felt? She didn't kill Amber, but she didn't try to stop Echo either.

"Hey, you still with me?" X asked, concerned.

"Yeah, yeah, I'm here," I said before I could get further lost in my own head. "Any idea on how to get out of here?"

I gave the inside of my cell a closer look. No furniture, the only light that came into the room was light from the moon and stars. The illumination came just outside my cell through the barred window.

The room stank of stale water. If I listened hard, I could hear a constant drip coming from one of the ends of the room.

"Let's take a closer look," X said, activating my night vision.

I searched the room through golden vision. It didn't tell me much. The farthest corners of the room cloaked in shadow were the same as the ones I could see to my right and left. They were made of thick grey stone. No way in, no way out.

A small puddle of water gathered at the left side of

the cell. The door to the cell was a steel plate reinforced with rivets. A sliding square window to see in and out of was closed at the moment.

"We have to get out of these chains first, or at least detach them from the ceiling," X pointed out. "Let me take a closer look at the chain and the anchor holding them into the ceiling."

I complied, moving my eyes over the links of the chain slowly before examining the iron anchor attaching them to the ceiling. There were four heavy screws holding each of the chains in place.

"Our best chance at the moment will be—"

X didn't get to finish her sentence. A heavy bolt on the other end of the cell moved free. The door swung open a second later to reveal a tall woman with red hair.

Sam entered the room. She wore brown boots and pants with a white shirt. Her red hair fell freely down her back. A knife sat snug against her left hip. She was more muscular than I saw in Echo's dream. She hadn't lightened up on her training in the slightest. If anything, she was even more athletic than before, like she was training for something or someone.

The door to the cell closed behind her with a hard bang. The steel lock was set in place once more.

"I knew they would send someone sooner or later.

With their resources, they can find almost anyone given enough time," Sam said, crossing her arms. She stood a safe distance away from me. "I just didn't think it would be you. Not after what they did to Amber. Echo or Preacher maybe, but not you."

"This isn't what you think," I said, shaking my head. I spat the sour taste out of my mouth again. "I'm not here to kill you. Immortal Corp didn't send me. What did you inject me with anyway? It tastes like rancid sugar."

"A neurotoxin that would keep you unconscious until your body healed itself enough to fight off the effects," Sam said raising an eyebrow at me. "You killed people in that bar, and I have two dozen wounded. And I'm supposed to believe you when you say you didn't come here to kill me? That's exactly what I would say if I were in your position."

"They didn't give me a chance. Anyone who died was killed by rogue fire from your own side," I said, shaking my head. "I didn't want to fight, but the orders you gave them didn't leave a whole lot of options. I'm not here for you, Sam. I don't know how you're going to believe me, but you have to trust me on this. I'm here to talk to you about Amber, about why she died, about taking down Immortal Corp."

This got a reaction out of her. Now instead of one

eyebrow raising, both did. We stood there staring at one another as she decided what to do with me.

"I didn't kill Amber," Sam said. "I want you to know I didn't kill her, but neither did I try and stop it. That is something I will regret until the day I die. I should have tried to stop it."

I swallowed hard. I wasn't exactly the emotional type, but everything inside the core of my being told me Sam was someone I could trust. She was a sister. Even though I didn't have memories of us coming up together, it was like my spirit knew and understood who she was.

"I lost my memory five years ago," I said, trying to figure out where to even begin telling Sam what had happened to me. "I'm still not sure how it happened. All I know is I spent five years not knowing who or what I was. Over the last few days, I've been finding out and—well, all roads have led me to you for more answers."

Sam chewed on her bottom lip.

"I'm not here because I was sent by Immortal Corp or my own revenge," I continued. Sam was on a teetering point between whether she was going to believe me or not. I needed something to push her over. "I just want answers. I want to make whoever is responsible for killing Amber pay, but most of all, I want her death to mean something. She may be gone, but her spirit will live on. I swear that much."

"Can't kill our spirit," Sam said, nodding slowly.

"Can't kill our spirit." I repeated the Pack Protocol mantra. "Help me find a way to honor her death. Please."

That was enough to send Sam over the edge. She nodded, slowly removing the blade from her sheath.

"I want you to know that if everything you said is the truth and you did forget who you were that when we trained I was always better than you at hand-to-hand combat," Sam said, eyeing me seriously. "If you try anything, I won't hesitate to sever your head from your body. Do you understand me, Danny?"

"No tricks," I told her. "I'm not here for a fight. I'm here to talk."

Sam nodded again. She took a step forward as if she were going to release me from my chains then hesitated.

"Before I get you down, I want to know as much as you do what happened to you?" Sam asked. "Where have you been for the last five years?"

"I'll tell you everything I know," I said.

The next half hour, I told her all that I remembered. She would ask a question here or there, but for the most part remained content to let me explain.

I started back at waking up in the alley on the moon with nothing more than my name. I told her about Wesley Cage and Echo, about the Reapers and Phoenix and finally about delving into Echo's memory.

Sam let out a low whistle when I was finished.

"Sounds like you've been through the meat grinder, Danny," Sam said, walking over to me. She sheathed her knife then took a key from her pocket. One, then the other, she let me go from my chains.

"Thanks," I said, massaging my wrists. "Sorry I had to find you like this."

"It's my fault for thinking that members of the Pack were beyond absolution," Sam said. "I should have known better. Amber changed and I followed in her footsteps. I'm glad you've found a different path as well."

I nodded.

"I told you everything I know," I said, rubbing the sleep from my eyes. I had no idea what time it was, but it had to be sometime early in the morning. "I could use some answers myself."

"Let's get you out of this cell and maybe some food in that black hole you call a stomach," Sam said with the first smile I'd seen yet. "Some things never change. I can hear it rumbling from here."

Sam pounded a very precise code on the closed door. "You can let us out. He's safe now."

The door swung outward.

Sam motioned to me. "Come on, Daniel, you've waited long enough for answers. It's time you had them."

CHAPTER FOURTEEN

SAM LED me with a quartet of guards to her home. We walked down the well-kept clean streets. The sun was just beginning to rise over the horizon. I received glares from a few of the guards while others looked at me with a mix of awe and suspicion.

I guess I couldn't expect much else. I had just cut through a number of their own like a buzz saw. Even if I had no other choice and I hadn't directly been the executioner, the dead were dead and there was no going back now.

We left Cecile's main street and made a hard left. At the end of the path, a large house stood with four white pillars in front. It wasn't quite a mansion but larger than most of the houses I had yet to see.

"When I liberated the city of Cecile from a gang

that had taken over called the Skull Bearers, it wasn't much more than a dirt road and a few shacks," Sam said, looking at the well-maintained street and homes on either side. "I didn't come here thinking I was going to improve the life of the community, but I guess life has a funny way of taking you down roads you didn't intend."

I nodded silently, sensing she wasn't done talking.

"We worked hard over the years to make the city something better," Sam said with a sigh of weary pride. "The rival gangs in the Badlands have left us alone for the most part. What I did to them when I first came hasn't been easily forgotten. Anyone who comes here now looking for trouble is dealt with quickly and brutally. Pretty much everyone who lives here is a trained warrior."

We reached the end of the road and Sam's home.

"Peso," Sam said, looking at the guard on my right. He was a hard-nosed man with grizzle over his jaw. "Can you return Daniel's gear and weapon to him? Let the others know he's a friend and can be trusted."

"Yes-yes, ma'am," Peso said with a sharp nod. He eyed me one more time then left with the other guards down the street.

"I don't think he likes me much," I said.

"He will, give him time," Sam answered. "I'll

address the rest of them tomorrow. Giving them standing orders to kill any stranger with a wolf tattoo on their left shoulder was a mistake. I'll deal with the fallout. That's on me."

Sam led me through the front door. Wood floors covered the inside of the house with brown furniture that matched and tall white walls. A staircase on the right opened up, leading to the upper floor, while a hall led deeper into the house.

Sam motioned me forward, taking the lead down the hall to a wide open room that was half kitchen, half living room.

"We'll get you food and answers and then you can sleep until your heart's content," Sam said, going over to the pantry and taking out an assortment of ingredients. She made me a meal while she told me the story I so desperately wanted to hear.

I pulled up a stool to the counter island and listened to a tale that felt so familiar.

"We were just kids when they recruited us," Sam said as she worked on the sandwich in front of her. "Well, most of us were. Preacher was the only exception. They promised us purpose, stability, and family. And for a time, they gave us just that. You don't remember any of those years? The tests, the training?"

"Nothing," I said, my mouth watering for the food

she was preparing as my mind watered for more of my past.

"We tested and trained year after year until they turned our bodies into super weapons and honed our fighting ability to needle-sharp points. There were seven of us all together: you, me, Amber, Preacher, Echo, Spartan, and Angel. You still like spread and spice in your sandwich?"

"Yeah, I like it all," I said, finding it strange and somehow wonderful that someone, anyone knew what I enjoyed to eat. "Keep going. What was I like?"

"No offense," Sam said, passing me a monster sandwich on a plate with a side of chips and a pickle. "You were kind of a scrawny kid. You were depressed, struggled with anxiety, the works. You had the right spirit, though. There was no denying that. We all did. That's what saw us through the training. Through those rough years of practice and drills and more practice and more drills."

I bit into the sandwich, forcing myself to eat and swallow before biting again and again. The food was great. Sam knew what she was doing around a sandwich.

"We went on missions for Immortal Corp," Sam said with a heavy sigh. "We thought we were working for the good guys, but the honest truth is, we'll never know how many of those people we killed were innocent and how many were guilty. To be honest with you, I don't want to know."

Sam paused, taking time to make her own sandwich.

"Maybe it's not such a bad thing you don't remember all of it," Sam said, slicing the meat with her knife. "Maybe it's a blessing in disguise. I can still see their faces. I can hear them plead and scream as we cut them down. Every night, every night."

"You didn't—we didn't know," I said, pausing between mouthfuls of food. "How could we have known? I have bits and pieces of when Wesley recruited me. He seemed like a good guy who actually cared. When he came to me on the moon, I got that same feeling."

"Cage wasn't like any of the other handlers," Sam said around a mouthful of food. "He was the best of them. I think he did actually care about doing some good. Maybe he was used by Immortal Corp just as much as we were. So yeah, there are more details we can go over, whatever you want to know, but those are the key points."

"Can you tell me about Amber?" I asked hesitantly. It was a conversation I mostly wanted to know, although there was a strong voice in my head telling me not to do it.

"Amber was a firework," Sam said, finishing her sandwich and taking the plates to clean. "She had this smile that made you feel like you were the most important person in the world. Her capacity to love is what made her the first to open her eyes and see what was really going on. You two were great together."

"The Order." I furrowed my brow, trying to remember what I knew from Echo's memory. "The heads of Immortal Corp, those three shadow figures on the screens. They're the ones who ordered you to kill Amber because she was trying to bring peace with the Order?"

"We mostly took our orders from handlers like Wesley Cage," Sam said, pouring us both a glass of water. She handed me mine then drained her own. "As far as I know, no one has ever seen the identity of the three on the screens. They only came by to give us orders of the utmost importance. In my years with Immortal Corp, I have only seen them twice. The second time was when they ordered me to kill Amber. I don't know who they are."

"You don't, but a handler like Wesley Cage might," I mused out loud.

"Maybe," Sam said, looking out the window at the

rising sun. "You know, I look out this window every day telling myself that I'm not that same animal they tried to turn us into. I tell myself that I'm making up for my past sins by helping this city. But I know it's only a matter of time before my past comes to catch up with me. If you were able to find me, they will too. Or maybe they already know where I am."

"I'm not telling anyone where you are, if that's what you're worried about," I said. "But I agree, if Wesley Cage was able to find me, then they'll find you sooner or later."

"I've got more to lose now," Sam said, biting her lip. "I have a city that will fight with me, but a city might not be enough to fend off Immortal Corp."

"What about Phoenix?" I asked. "They have an army. Not only an army, they're trying to bring about a real lasting peace and a new chance for Earth."

"Phoenix, huh?" Sam looked over at me with that raised eyebrow of hers. "You a rebel for the good guys now?"

"Maybe I'm just tired of being a tool for the bad guys," I said. "I made a promise to help someone from Phoenix get her father back. After that, I'm on my own. I'm going to keep getting answers to my past and take down Immortal Corp while I'm at it."

Sam let out a low whistle. "Taking down Immortal

Corp is going to be easier said than done. They're massive, well-funded, and have a heritage that goes back centuries."

"I've got to," I said. "The more I find out about them, the more I understand what I have to do. For me, for Amber, for what they did to us."

"I'd help you, but—"

Slapping bare feet on the wood caught my ear. Not just walking but running. Someone was sprinting toward us down the hall.

CHAPTER FIFTEEN

SAM MOVED FASTER than I did, going to the entrance to the hall and crouching down with her arms open. A ball of dark red hair and energy slammed into her with a hug.

"Momma, Momma." The little girl hugged Sam tightly around her neck. "I'm hungry, I'm hungry."

"Well, of course you are," Sam said, smiling as she lifted the girl off the floor. "You're always hungry. Hey, I have someone I want you to meet."

The little girl pulled back from her mom and looked at me for the first time. She smiled shyly then nuzzled her head against her mother's chest.

"Daniel, I'd like you to meet my daughter, Amber," Sam said, looking at me. She then turned to the little girl. "Amber, this is Daniel, he's—he's your uncle."

My eyes were wide. I was unsure how to process any of this. Not only did Sam have a daughter, but she named her after Amber and she introduced me as family.

"Uh—hi, hey there," I said, offering a handshake.

Do kids even shake hands? I asked myself. *How am I supposed to say hello? Do I call her my niece if I was introduced as her uncle?*

"I'm shy," Amber said, burying her face in Sam again.

"Oh please, that's a first." Sam laughed out loud. "Come on, be polite. Say hello."

"Hello," Amber managed from behind two chunky hands she put over her face.

I dropped my offered hand, feeling like an idiot. My expression must have said it all because Sam went on to take control of the situation.

"I never thought a life like this could be mine," Sam said, slowly swaying as she held her daughter. "I know I don't deserve this, but I'm prepared to protect it now with everything I've got."

I nodded, understanding everything Sam wasn't saying. She was prepared to sacrifice herself for her daughter. She wouldn't be coming with me after Immortal Corp. Maybe she would have walked that path before, but not now.

Seeing the joy in her face as she held her daughter to her chest, I didn't blame her. I couldn't blame her. Despite everything, I was actually happy for her.

"All right, munchkin." Sam kissed her daughter on her soft bed of dark red hair. "I'm going to sit you down so you can get some breakfast."

"No, hold me, hold me," Amber said, clinging to her mother.

"Come on, let me put you down just for a second." Sam laughed. "You said you're hungry. Let me get you some food."

The little girl seemed content with that trade-off.

Sam placed her on one of the stools around the kitchen island.

"I came here looking for a city to call my own," Sam explained. "What I found was something I wasn't ready for. I found a community and a family of my own. Her father's asleep upstairs. He's a good man, Daniel, not like us."

I ran my right hand through my short dark hair. There were words for a moment like this, but I couldn't find them.

"I'm happy for you, Sam," I said, meaning what I was saying. "I really am. I'm glad you were able to find this. I take it you named her Amber after—"

"That's right," Sam said, returning to her daughter

with some kind of protein pack in her hand and a glass of milk. "She's named Amber after her aunt. After the woman who was brave enough to be the first one to change."

Sam's daughter took the food with wide eyes and went to town on both the milk and the protein pack. She was small, but she could chow down in a hurry.

I rubbed my tired eyes, trying to remember when was the last time I slept. I had a few hours on the dropship and that had been it since the previous morning.

"You look like you're about to keel over," Sam said with a grin. "Come on, we have a spare downstairs bedroom where you can sleep. You can take a shower now or when you wake up. We'll talk more later."

I nodded dumbly, my eyes straying over to where Sam's daughter was bobbing up and down on her seat humming some tune I didn't know but sounded oddly familiar.

The little girl looked happy, lost in her own small world where there were no Cyber Hunters, Immortal Corp, or memories of death. I saw that innocence and something inside of me wanted to protect it as if I was actually her real uncle.

"Momma's going to be right back," Sam said to her

daughter. "Uncle Daniel needs to take a nap. I'm going to show him where to sleep."

"You're tired?" Amber said, looking up at me with wide eyes. "You take naps too?"

"I love naps," I told her with a smile. "I take them whenever I can get them."

"I don't like naps." Amber shook her head violently from side to side. "Uh, uh."

"I bet," I said with a grin. "You'll feel different when you're older. I guarantee it."

I followed Sam back down the hall toward the front door. We made a left past the stairs where another door greeted us. This room was like a hybrid guest room with a bathroom in the back.

"Get some rest, get cleaned up, and then we can talk some more," Sam told me. "I'll grab some of my husband's clothes and set them outside the door for you."

"Okay," I said, looking over the sparsely decorated yet inviting room. "Thank you."

"I'm glad you came," Sam said as she paused at the door. "I'm glad someone else made it out of Immortal Corp alive."

With that, she closed the door behind her, leaving me to my own thoughts.

I was dead tired, but the thought of going to sleep

in the clothes I wore was less than compelling. The white sheets on the guest bed led me straight to the shower.

The hot water felt like a gift. A bar of white soap stood ready on a recess in the shower like an alert guard ready for battle.

I scrubbed the dirt and grime off my face, hair, and the rest of my body as I thought about everything Sam had been through. Her path from Immortal Corp had been so different from my own.

Still, here we were now. Our common bond had brought us together again. That was four members of the Pack. I had come face to face with Echo and Sam. I had learned about Amber and a dream told me a little bit about Preacher. The man called Spartan and the woman named Angel were the last two I had yet to meet or remember.

As far as I knew, both of them along with Preacher, still worked for Immortal Corp. I'd have to go through them one day. Maybe they'd already been sent out like Echo and were looking for me.

I shut off the steaming water after rinsing off the soap. I towel dried then wrapped it around my waist. Going to the door of my room, I cracked it open. Sure enough, there was a pile of clean clothes by the foot of the door.

The pants were tight and the shirt a size too small, but I wasn't going to complain. I threw myself on the bed, thinking it was the most comfortable thing I'd ever lain on.

"How are you holding up?" X asked.

She had been quiet since the interrogation with Sam, the trip to her house and the conversation thereafter.

"I think we're going to be okay," I said, closing my eyes. I already felt sleep beckoning to me. "How're you holding up?"

"Oh you know, like an AI implant in a super soldier mercenary," X teased. "I'm all right, thanks for asking."

"Why wouldn't I?" I asked her. "I'm only here because of you."

"What do you mean?" X asked.

"I mean you've saved my mercenary rear end more than a few times already," I said with eyes closed. "I'd be lost without you, X."

I don't remember if X said more. I fell into a deep sleep that lasted for hours. When I finally did wake up, the large windows with the drawn blinds showed moonlight around the edges.

I yawned, feeling rejuvenated but once again hungry.

"How long did I sleep?" I asked out loud.

"All day," X answered. "It's okay. You needed it."

"Man," I said, swinging my legs off the bed and getting my bearings. "And now I'm hungry again."

"You have a day left to get whatever answers you need," X reminded me. "The dropship comes in twenty-four hours."

"Right," I said, pushing myself off the bed and walking to the bedroom door. "Food first and then more info from Sam."

"You're not going to ask her to come with you, are you?" X asked. "I mean, not with what she has here now."

"No way," I said. "Sam's found something special here. I'm not going to be the one to break that apart. Besides, I already have a partner."

"Who me?" X asked. I could hear the smile in her tone.

"That's right," I said.

I opened the bedroom door and walked out into the hall.

A blond man had just come in through the front door. He was a bit taller than I was and skinnier. He looked surprised for a second then gave me a smile.

"You must be Daniel, Samantha's friend," he said, extending a hand in my direction. "I actually just came in to see if you were awake. The girls are outside. I'm Gavin."

"Gavin," I said, shaking his hand. "Thank you for having me in your home."

"You're welcome to stay as long as you'd like," Gavin said, holding my eye. He also held on to my hand a second longer. "Samantha is a great woman. Whatever it is you came here to talk to her about, talk about it, but leave her out of whatever it is that's going on. She's happy."

Gavin's stare was intense but not intimidating. I got what he was saying. I knew a half dozen ways to kill him right there in the hallway. The fever in his eyes told me he'd die happily if it meant protecting his wife.

"I'm not asking her to go anywhere," I said, pulling my hand back. "I just came here for some answers. I've got most of them. I'll be leaving tomorrow night."

Gavin let out an audible sigh. Relief crossed his face.

"I'm sorry. I'm sorry if I came across as intimidating," Gavin shook his head. "It's just that—Samantha doesn't talk about her past a whole lot. Over the years, I've gathered she was part of some dark stuff. I don't want her to get pulled back into that."

I was still trying to get over the fact that Gavin

thought he was intimidating. Apparently, I wasn't the only one.

"Did this guy just say he was sorry for coming across as intimidating?" X said in my head. "Sorry, I had to say something."

Gavin's tight pants, boots, and tighter shirt didn't exactly help his claim.

"It's okay," I told him. "I wasn't intimidated. Sam's happy here. I'm not going to get in the way of that."

"Really, you weren't intimidated at all?" Gavin asked with a sideways look. "I've been told I carry a certain air at times. It's okay if you were just a little bit scared. I already apologized for it."

"Not even the slightest," I told him.

"Hmmm," Gavin said, breaking into a smile. "Well, come on outside. Samantha and Amber are looking at the moon. It's kind of their nightly routine."

I joined Gavin as we stepped outside the front door onto the porch. The sky looked incredible. The clouds had moved and now a million tiny lights shone down on us along with the giant silver ball we called the moon.

Sam stood with Amber in her arms, looking up at the sky in wonder. Gavin and I moved to join them.

"Daniel, there's something wrong," X said inside

my head. "Contact coming down the street at a run. He doesn't look happy."

I concentrated on turning on my night vision. X was right. From the main road, someone turned the corner and was coming down the street at a dead sprint. I couldn't tell if he had any weapons at this distance, but I wasn't going to take the chance.

"Sam," I said, stepping in front of the family to shield Amber and Gavin as best I could. If anything was fired at us, Sam would be able to heal, but the other two wouldn't.

The warning in my voice said it all. Sam followed my gaze, handing Amber over to Gavin. Her right hand went for the sheathed blade in her right boot.

"It's okay, it's one of ours," Sam said, squinting into the darkness. "It's Peso. How-how did you see that far in the dark?"

I didn't have to answer her question. Peso came up to us at a skid. He was out of breath but still managed to relay his message.

"Skull Bearers—and the Krull—from the east," Peso gasped. "They'll be here by morning."

CHAPTER SIXTEEN

I HAD no idea what Peso was gasping about, but apparently, everyone else did.

"I'm going to take Amber inside," Gavin said. "Be careful, my love."

"I will," Sam said, leaning back to give her husband and daughter a kiss.

"Momma, what's wrong? No, Momma," Amber said, confused. She didn't know what was going on, but she knew enough that something was very wrong.

"Shhh," Gavin told his daughter as he walked back inside. He patted her little back gently. "Momma has to go to work for a bit. She'll be right back."

"Catch your breath," Sam told Peso. "How do you know?"

"Scouts just came back," Peso said, finally getting control of his breathing. "They've seen the Skull Bearers and the Krull mobilizing. Intel says they're headed here and will be in the city come first light."

"I thought you killed the Skull Bearers when you took over Cecile?" I asked Sam, trying to remember correctly. "And who are the Krull?"

"I killed who I had to, to make a statement that the city was mine," Sam said with a pained expression on her face. Apparently, remembering her past sins was more uncomfortable than I guessed. "Those members of the gang who were willing to leave I allowed to do so. They took refuge in surrounding cities. We've had incidents pop up over the years, but nothing like this."

"The Krull are another rival gang. They're mutated humans who live in the caves of the Badlands. Usually, they're too small to cause any real issues on their own, but now that they've joined forces with the remainder of the Skull Bearers, they're coming with almost a hundred warriors strong." Peso answered my next question. "They have vehicles. They are well-armored and carry weapons. Nothing major, but enough small arms fire to kill everyone in Cecile if we let it happen."

"Well, good thing we're not going to let it happen," Sam said. She addressed Peso with no hesitation at all in her voice. "Get the noncombatants to the bunker.

Mobilize the city force then come get me. I'll be in the armory."

"Understood," Peso said. Without another word, he ran to obey.

"You should leave," Sam said, looking over at me. "This isn't your fight. I can't help you in yours. You don't have to help me fight mine."

"Riiiiight," I said, tilting my chin down and looking at her with the tops of my eyes. "You're going to show me that adorable kid you named Amber then tell me I can go along my way and run from a fight? Not a chance. I actually have a crazy idea."

"You, a crazy idea?" Sam said, grinning in the dark. "Let's talk while we walk."

Sam led me down the street back to the main road. I pitched my plan to her as we traveled through the small town of Cecile.

There wasn't a lot of activity on the street. It was late. There were a few lights on in windows and the sounds of the bar down the road alive with subdued chatter.

"What if we have a chance for a little redemption here?" I said, sharing my plan with Sam. "Enough of your people have suffered. You and I can fight the battle they can't without fear of dying ourselves."

"I mean, I like it, but you understand we're not one

hundred percent immortal, right?" Sam said with a signature eyebrow raise. "Decapitation, drowning, burned until there's nothing left are all ways for us to die."

We stopped in front of a one-story building where two city guards nodded to Sam and moved out of the way. They eyed me with a look of half disdain, half fear.

Sam pressed a digital code into the magnetic door lock. It beeped with a faint click. The door swung open. Motion sensors detected our presence and lit the room with brilliant white light.

I had to do a double take. I didn't expect the town of Cecile to have more than a handful of weapons, let alone armaments of this size or technology. Racks upon racks of firearms ranging from heavy rocket launchers to light blasters and bladed weapons lined the walls and shelves. It was almost hard to walk in the place.

"Hey, don't judge," Sam said, entering the room. "Everyone needs a hobby."

"I didn't say anything," I said, admiring the collection. "But back to the plan. I think we can take these Skull Bearers and Krull ourselves."

Sam went to the far end of the room, where a high

tech metal recurve bow rested on the wall. She handled it with care, mulling over my plan.

"Peso said there were nearly a hundred of them," Sam said out loud. "We won't get out of the fight unscathed, but we can take them. It may not be pretty. There's a one hundred percent chance we'll get wounded and pain will come with that."

"Physical pain doesn't do a whole lot for me these days," I told her. "There are things much worse than that."

Sam slowly nodded. "I can order the rest of the civilian force out of the city, giving us free rein. We can be guaranteed of no collateral damage. Maybe we can wipe a little red off our ledger."

"If there's a chance, I think we owe it to our pasts to try," I said. "Besides, you said you were better in a fight than I am. I'd like to see it and prove you wrong."

Sam barked a laugh. A genuine smile came to her face. "Just like the old days. It's good to have you back, Danny. I'll tell Peso the plan. Help yourself to anything you like. Your own weapons and armor are in the corner."

"Will do," I said, heading for the far side of the room as Sam headed for the front door.

"You remember what your callsign was when we

went on missions?" Sam said as if an afterthought. She stood by the door, about to leave. "Mine was Red. Inventive, right?"

"I should have guessed." I looked at her, waiting for her to continue.

"You were 'Savage,' Daniel," Sam said, remembering exactly why. "Not because you were the strongest or the fastest, but because you could take the most damage, recover the fastest, and keep going."

There was a level of respect in her words as she remembered so many past missions that were lost to my own memory. Sam gave me a final nod then left the room.

"Savage, huh?" X said out loud. "Should have known. You think you two will be able to take a small army by yourselves? I understand you're trying to save lives, but is that even achievable? I mean, I've run the numbers and your success rate for two individuals to take on nearly one hundred is point zero, zero, one, seven, five."

"Never tell me the odds, X," I said, going over to the corner of the room where my scorched Phoenix armor and my MK II sat. "I don't do statistics."

"Hey, I'm with you no matter what," X answered "Just want you to make an informed decision."

"Roger that," I said, strapping myself into the lightweight armor. "Any suggestions for some additional weapons besides the MK II?"

"The strategy you used in the bar seemed to meet your fighting style almost perfectly," X thought out loud. "You'll need something heavy to deal with the vehicles coming in the city, but after that, if you can get in close, a pair of bladed weapons would do you the most good."

I clipped the chest plate into place, looking around the room so X could take further inventory of the place.

"On the far end, see those knives and axes?" X asked.

I followed her instruction, looking over at the shelf. There was an assortment of knives ranging from throwing blades no longer than my pointer finger to near swords that spanned the length of my forearm.

"Choose a midsize one," X instructed. "It should be sharp on one side and serrated on the other. Next grab one of those axes. You don't need it to be huge. Something that can also be thrown will be most advantageous in a fight."

I obeyed X's advice, choosing a black-bladed knife I clipped onto the front of my belt along with an axe with a slightly curved handle. The axe had a blade on one end and a dull hammer-like edge on the other.

"Next you'll need something big to take out any vehicles," X said. "There's a Valkyrie Z9 on the wall. The big one with the tube for a rifle end, can't miss it."

"This thing is like a rocket launcher," I said, going over to the impressive weapon. "Are you sure this isn't overkill?"

"It'll bring a steady laser beam to cut through their armor and vehicles," X instructed. "Guaranteed to do the job."

"If you say so," I said, hefting the heavy weapon off the wall.

"Peso doesn't like it, but he has his orders," Sam said, once again entering the room. "I have food on the way as well. Figured you be hungry."

"I'm always hungry," I said with a grin.

Sam nodded in agreement with the weapons I had chosen. She looked at my hip where I carried my MK II.

"Still appreciate the older weapons, huh?" Sam said, nodding down to the hand cannon. "You know the MK II was a low round caliber weapon in the old days."

"I've read about it," I said. "I just liked it for its

accuracy and reliability. The drum you see on it now is an upgrade I got from Phoenix."

"Fancy," Sam said with approval. She made her way into the room going to a case on the floor at the end of the first aisle. She knelt down, allowing the case to scan her eyes. It clicked open.

Sam began taking out her own body armor. She wore a suit of lightweight armor in a gunmetal color. Shin guards, vambraces, and a steel chest plate accompanied a helmet with a V-shaped visor for her to see through.

We made quite the pair. Two runaway mercenaries from a private company's experiment box.

Sam completed her arsenal with a quiver of arrows with a variety of different tips, from syringes to explosives. She carried two long knives in a sheath at her lower back and a belt of grenades.

"You think Gavin is going to just stand by and let you do all the fighting?" I asked, remembering Sam's husband who fancied himself the intimidating type. "He doesn't strike me as the guy that's going to stand by."

"He will for our daughter," Sam said, motioning me to follow her out the door. "He's a good man, he's loving, kind, and a great father but among his many attributes is not the mentality of a fighter. Maybe that's why I love him so much. He's everything we're not."

I followed Sam out into the dark city. Nearly every house was lit now as the city militia went from home to home evacuating the city in the dead of night.

Peso and Gavin approached us from the street. The former looked hurried, the latter worried.

"We'll get everyone out safe," Peso said. "Please reconsider allowing the city militia to stay and fight."

"You have your orders," Sam said without blinking. She turned to Gavin. "Amber?"

"She's safe, with Karen and the others. They can protect her. Let me fight by your side this time. You have nothing to prove. You've done enough for this city, for all of us."

"My darling," Sam said, going to her husband and placing a hand on his cheek. "I'll fight with a free mind knowing our daughter is under your care."

Gavin's jaw clenched. I could tell he wanted to say more, but there was no argument that he could pose that would make sense for him to fight and for Sam to stay behind. She was a genetically engineered super soldier who healed at an unnatural rate. There weren't a whole lot of reasons for her not to fight.

Peso looked like he was going to argue some more then glanced at me for help.

"Sorry, amigo," I said. "She's right. We can do this, just the two of us without anyone else having to die. Well, not anyone in Cecile. The Skull Bearers and the Krull are about to make the worst mistake of their lives."

CHAPTER SEVENTEEN

THE SUN WAS JUST CRESTING the horizon. Sam and I knew what direction the attack would be coming from. The road east of the city was as pristine as all the others. I was still getting over how strange it looked. A well-paved road going out from the tiny city to be lost in the seemingly endless desert terrain.

We had taken up spots opposite the road from one another. Sam was across the street in a two-story building with a balcony. She hunched low, staying out of sight. Her bow rested on her knee, her helmet beside her.

I had chosen the ground floor on a single-story building across the street. A porch gave me a moderate amount of protection. I found a rocking chair there and sat talking to Sam over the earpiece I had been given. We talked about who we were, who I had been.

"I'm still surprised you haven't asked me about those tattoos of yours," Sam said around a mouthful of the hot breakfast provided for us. "You'd think you'd want to know about those."

"Oh, I do," I said, lowering the lukewarm tin cup of caf from my lips. The stuff was so strong, it gave me goosebumps. I loved it. "Tattoos were next on the unanswered agenda. There's a lot for me to get through these days."

"You got a tattoo every time we completed a mission," Sam explained. "I thought you were crazy. I mean, we completed every single mission. There was no room for failure and we didn't take defeat for an answer. I guess looking back, it was smart. Now you at least have a painted history of what you've been through."

"Yeah, it doesn't do me a whole lot of good these days since I can't remember any of the missions we went on," I answered. "The only tattoo I have any kind of meaning to now is the wolf on my left shoulder, and that's it."

"We weren't on all the missions together, but I'll write down what I remember and see if we can place the corresponding tattoo to that outing," Sam answered. "There was this one time on the moon we were sent to take out a new kingpin who had popped up pushing some state-of-the-art drug. Not sure why Immortal Corp wanted him out, but you and I were sent in to take care of it. I remember when it was over you got an ancient helmet on the back of your right arm with the words 'Do not go gentle'."

I looked down at the back of my right arm. Instinct more than anything else made me perform the action. It wasn't like I could see anything. I was dressed and I wore the same Phoenix light armor I arrived with.

"Do not go gentle," I repeated the words. "Sounds like me."

"That's you in a nutshell." Sam laughed out loud. She paused after a long sigh. "Thank you, Daniel."

"For what?" I asked.

"For helping me protect my family, for not asking me to go with you when this is all done," Sam whispered.

"Your family's going to be safe," I said, shifting uncomfortably. I didn't do well with praise apparently. "Those bunkers you had prepared under the city was a smart move."

"There weren't enough of them, though," Sam said with a sigh. "We had to send half the city out into the hills north of here. The militia will protect them."

"You did what you could and this city is better for having you," I answered, trying to pull Sam's mind to something else before she had time to dwell on her past sins. "Tell me the plan again. There are mines on the road out there?"

"I figured when we paved the streets, it would be important to build in mines. I mean, why not? It was only a matter of time before someone tried to take back Cecile," Sam said. "They'll attack us head on, relying on their numbers and vehicles. Plus, they're not the sharpest tools in the shed, if you know what I mean. We'll wait until they're close, right in the middle of the minefield a hundred meters from our location. When I detonate the mines, we'll have to take out whatever's left standing in front of us. It'll take time for the vehicle behind the mines to maneuver around the wreckage. Once we do, we can deal with them."

"Simple enough," I said, rocking slowly back and forth in my chair. Something caught my eye. An image in the distance, maybe a mirage.

"You see them?" Sam asked. "They're here."

I looked across the street up into the building's balcony. Sam was in the process of placing her helmet over her head and stringing her bow. She looked as intimidating as the grim reaper herself. I guessed that was the point. Blood-red hair fell back from her helmet. She nocked an arrow.

"You remember our mantra?" Sam asked. "Our pack code?"

"Echo reminded me of it," I said.

"They can kill our bodies," Sam said almost reverently.

"But they can't kill our spirit," I finished.

The comm line we used to speak went quiet.

I lifted the Valkyrie V9 to my shoulder. It was a heavy son of a gun with a cross at the end of the barrel meant for crosshairs. The seconds ticked by and the images of vehicles became clearer.

They were what I had expected. After my run-in with Papa and the Reapers, I knew what kinds of vehicles these gangs used. Beat-up rusted cars and trucks, basically anything that would move on wheels. Along with them came a dozen or more dirt bikes and sand buggies.

I didn't think Peso was lying, but I did think he had a problem counting. He had said there were just under a hundred. The group quickly approaching looked well over that. Maybe even double that number.

The lead vehicle was a truck with an open bed. Two flags flew from it. One I could make an intelligent guess stood for the Skull Bearers. It was a white human skull with a brown background.

The other flag slapping in the wind was some kind of insect, maybe the prongs of a beetle. The pincers were black on a green background.

"I know you don't want the odds," X said in my head. "But that's way more than a hundred. You want a head count?"

"Please," I asked quietly so the comms channel wouldn't pick up my words and relay it to Sam. "How many?"

"I count a hundred and fifty-nine," X said. "Intel on the small weapons was correct. I'm not getting any eviscerating mortars or super cannons. You might have a few flamethrowers or grenades in there, though."

"We can deal with that," I said, taking in a long, deep breath through my nose and exhaling through my mouth. I spoke in a regular voice so Sam could hear me now. "You ready for this?"

"I'm going to let them come as close as I can before we hit them," Sam said. "You take out the first wave of their vehicles with that Valkyrie V9 of yours. I have explosive arrows ready to get any of the stragglers."

"You got it," I said as the front truck bearing the flags roared down at us.

I crouched behind the waist-high rail of the porch I

was on. It wasn't much cover, but maybe with the way the shadow covered me, I'd be able to stay hidden just as long as I needed.

The truck was so close now, I could make out people inside the cab and on the back. If "people" was the right word at all. I remembered the conversation about the Krull being mutated humans. I just didn't think they'd look this bad. Some of these guys could do with a major makeover.

Eyes too big for their head and missing patches of hair were the first signs there was something very seriously wrong. Arms too long for their bodies and violent curvatures of their spines confirmed this.

They were fifty meters from us and closing. They started to holler and whoop, pointing at Sam's location.

I looked up to see her. She was a sight. Sam stood upright with no fear in the world. She had her right foot on the railing in front of her. Her bow was drawn back taut. The breeze caught her crimson hair, splaying it out behind her like a cape.

"Hey, you going to detonate the mines?" I asked, sighting down the barrel of my weapon. "They're so close, I can see the raw meat hanging from the driver's teeth."

"No mercy," Sam said so cold, so quiet, I said a

silent prayer of thanks she was on my side. "Kill them all."

The explosion that erupted in the center of their convoy line was closer and more violent than I anticipated. I'm not sure how many mines Sam stacked under her road, but it was enough to leave a crater and rip through a good third if not more of their number.

Flaming vehicles catapulted through the sky in slow motion. My ears rang from the sound of the detonation. A wave of heat hit my face.

Then it was all action and reaction.

I recovered, placing the Valkyrie on my shoulder and sighting down the barrel.

"Keep the trigger pulled. It'll take a second for the laser to fire," X said, coaching me on how to use the weapon. "Be prepared for a push on your shoulder."

I obeyed, keeping my right pointer finger on the trigger. I took aim on the lead vehicles that made it past the explosion. The truck was one of them, along with a handful of smaller vehicles and dirt bikes.

They were twenty meters and closing. If they spotted me hunched down behind the porch railing, they hadn't opened fire.

A golden laser shot out from the end of the Valkyrie V9 with a heavy hum. I felt pressure in my shoulder like the weapon was trying to push me back. I gritted my teeth and held my ground.

Trying to maneuver the beam was like holding a two-hundred-pound mutie on a leash and directing him where to go.

The beam ripped through anything it touched, both metal and flesh alike. I drew a slanted line right through the front truck, directly through the next car and decapitated a pair of dirt bikes with one sweep of the weapon.

Sam rained down fire on the vehicles closest to us with her arrows. Each time an arrow struck its target, it ended with an explosion consuming the enemy in a ball of flames.

I swept the Valkyrie V9 back and forth across the enemy lines. Anyone who got too close was dealt with by Sam.

We took them by surprise as we whittled down their numbers. The middle section of their convoy had fallen prey to the mines. The front had been taken so utterly off guard, we killed more than half of them before they were able to comprehend what was going on and run for cover.

The return fire was now coming from the rear third of the enemy force. This force had finally managed to maneuver around the wreckage the mines brought on.

The enemy fire wasn't accurate, but with this many soldiers, you didn't really have to be. The sheer volume of fire power had us pinned down. A second later, I got energy beams peppering my location and old school rounds took chunks off the wood building and railing around me.

I ripped through two more trucks loaded with the enemy before I had to pull back. A round clipped me in the chest and another slammed into my face.

The round that hit me in the cheek snapped my head back to the right. I stumbled for a second. Pain came hot and fierce as blood dripped down my armor.

I lost hold of the Valkyrie V9. I stumbled back over the porch and took cover round the side of the building.

"You good?" Sam asked over the sounds of weapons fire. "Daniel, are you okay?"

CHAPTER EIGHTEEN

THE PAIN in my jaw was excruciating. Despite this, I tried to respond. I knew what I wanted to say, but my jaw just wouldn't obey.

"Daniel," X said, her voice full of worry. "Your jaw's broken. I can respond to Sam for you if you're good with that."

I nodded, hearing motion from the far side of the building. Instinct dropped my hands to my belt. They came to rest on the axe and knife.

"Samantha," X said, connecting to the comm unit in my ear. "My name is X. I'm an AI in Daniel's head. No time to explain more now. He's okay. His jaw is broken, so he can't talk at the moment."

"Why wouldn't you just tell—never mind," Sam said with a grunt as an explosion went off somewhere on her end. "I'm going ground level. They're swarming the center of the street on foot. They're converging on your location."

"You get that?" X asked.

I nodded, trying to work my jaw, but all that came out was, "Yu."

That animal inside me came to the surface once more. I looked to my right as the first mutated soldier turned to point his blaster into the alley behind the house.

Speed, I reminded myself in my own mind. *You're faster than any of them. Speed, Daniel, be smart.*

The first mutie took my knife from the bottom of his chin through his mouth and into his skull. I swung around, doing a three-hundred-and-sixty-degree turn, planting my axe in the chest of the next mutie who rounded the corner.

A roll took me into the street and right into the center of their force.

As I did at the bar, I used their own numbers against them. I wheeled around with my axe and knife, striking out to the point I didn't even plan my next move. I only had time to react.

Somewhere in the background as the blood flew through the air like fine mist, I heard X coordinating with Sam.

"Samantha," X said. "He's in the center of the city street. We have a few dozen here, but there are more coming around the perimeter of the buildings as well."

"Understood," Sam said. "I'll take the group scouting the exterior of the buildings on my side of the street. Then circle back and give you a hand, two seconds."

I took a club to the side of my head then a round to my left calf that forced me to a knee. Some mutie thought he actually beat me. He roared with his twisted teeth and lifted his weapon over my head for what he thought would be a killing blow. The club was larger than my torso.

I rolled out of the way to create distance then hurled my knife at his throat. It landed with a wet thud. He looked stunned, grasping at the weapon, like that was going to help.

"Keep moving," X encouraged me. "You can do it. There're ten left in the center of the street. Keep moving!"

I was tired, beat up, but not broken, never broken. I lunged forward into a run, ripping the blade from the throat of the dying mutie as he fell to his knees.

Sam fell down somewhere beside me and landed with a blur of motion. Her bow was gone, but a knife in her right hand sliced the belly of one of her targets.

Her helmet was scratched. She wasn't moving her left leg very well, but that wasn't going to stop her.

We fought back to back. I tossed her my blade over my shoulder like we practiced the move before. Sam caught it and impaled a mutie Krull through the forehead.

I reached for my MK II and went to work. At such a short range, each shot was a kill. I decided to go with the tungsten steel bolts. The pieces of hardened metal were powerful enough to puncture bone and muscle, sometimes even ripping through one target completely and burying itself into another.

Against all odds, we were doing it. The dead were forming a circle around us.

"Axe," Sam yelled.

I didn't miss a beat. With my right hand still doling out death via the MK II, I flipped the weapon in my left hand so I caught the blade. I handed the weapon hilt first to Sam, who was still at my back.

A brute exited the alley in front of me at a run. He carried some kind of hose and tank behind him.

I was moving too fast to stop myself. I fired at him at close range before he could open up on us. As luck would have it, the mutie was caring a flamethrower. My tungsten steel bolt went through his body and punctured the tank.

The explosive force lifted me off my feet. A wave of heat washed over my face and body as I crashed down to the hard ground somewhere against a wooden railing.

Disoriented, I tried to get my bearings. The MK II was lost somewhere in the fall. I struggled to my feet, looking for Sam. She was a house away, not moving. A pool of blood came out from her helmet.

I don't know how many Skull Bearers and Krull we killed, but we hadn't killed enough. Survivors from the fight were struggling to their feet. There were a handful of them that went for Sam and another three who pointed their weapons at me.

Heavy weapon fire from some kind of laser repeater raked through the enemy. Whoever was behind the trigger wasn't going to win any awards for marksmanship. With the element of surprise and a weapon like that, they didn't have to be in line for marksman of the year.

I looked up to see Gavin with the repeater strapped to his shoulder. His face was a mask of fear and hate as he tore through both Badland factions. He walked forward, cutting them down with impunity. He made his way to my side without looking at me.

I could see everything in his eyes. I could see the memories and nightmares being made right now.

Memories and nightmares that he would carry with him for the rest of his life.

Then, from the corner of my eye, I saw a second mutie with a dented flamethrower strapped to his back. I was on the ground posing no real threat at the moment. The mutated human ignored me and focused on Gavin.

I knew what was about to happen. Gavin was about to get cooked alive. Sam was only just stirring. I lost my MK II in the last explosion. My knife and axe were gone. I couldn't even yell to warn Gavin. My jaw was still out of commission while my body healed over.

X saw the same thing. She tried to yell at him, to warn him. No use. He was too lost in the fog of war.

Past the pain, past all the discomfort and the brutality of the moment, I thought of Amber. Not my Amber; of Sam and Gavin's Amber. I thought of that little bundle of honest energy going through life without a father.

I was still getting to know what kind of man I was before. Honestly, I didn't know if I liked him or not. The man I was today, I knew well. And he wasn't going to let that little girl grow up without her dad no matter the cost.

I found my legs and lunged for Gavin. He still

didn't see the flame-throwing mutie coming at him from his left.

I grabbed Gavin, breaking him from his frozen state holding down the trigger of his repeater. I slammed him to the ground.

"Hey, what are you doing!?" Gavin yelled at me as I took him down.

I couldn't answer him if I wanted to.

"Get down!" X yelled at Gavin for me.

I hunched over Gavin, using my body as a shield.

The mutie with the flamethrower opened up, hosing us with a stream of white hot fire.

I was ready. I could take it.

The tongue of heat scorched my back armor, sending stabbing ice-cold pain through my back. The agony was something I had never experienced before.

I couldn't help it. My jaw wouldn't let me talk, but I sure as heck could roar. I lifted my head, bellowing my rage to the sky above. I spread my arms over Gavin's body, trying to protect as much of him as I could for as long as I could.

"X!" I managed to scream somehow despite my jaw. I didn't know what I expected her to do. It was just the first name that came to my mind. I turned my head to the left. I needed to try and protect X's data chip implanted behind my right ear from the incoming flames.

"Oh, Daniel! Daniel!" X screamed in my head. "Hold on. Sam's getting up. You hold on!"

I couldn't feel my body anymore. I was fading quick. Even I knew the human body can only handle so much pain before it falls into an unconscious state.

Gavin struggled underneath me to get away from the flames, maybe to get up and try to help, I didn't know.

Images of my Amber raced through my mind. I could see her there smiling, almost welcoming me to come with her.

What was it Sam had said earlier? My addled mind tried to form the coherent thought. *Enough fire was a way to kill us?*

"Daniel, don't go!" X yelled in my head. "She's here! She's here!"

Suddenly, I was back on the main street of Cecile. I felt numb, but the constant licks of flame serrating my back were gone. I fell backward and onto my left side, unable to move.

I could see the still wounded Sam taking down the mutie with the flamethrower. She ran her knife across both his wrists, severing any way for him to hold the weapon. He dropped it, screaming in pain.

Sam's helmet had been ripped off or maybe she had taken it off. Her face was red with a sheet of her own blood, but I saw her eyes. Rage was the best way for me to describe them.

Sam lifted her head to the heavens and let out something that sounded more animal than woman. She stuck that mutie with her knife a half dozen times in the side of his head and neck.

Dark blood poured from the mutie in streams. She didn't stop stabbing him either, even when he fell to his knees. With a few more deep slashes and a sawing motion at the end, she took his head from his lifeless body.

The mutie fell headless to the ground. I could see a few of our surviving attackers helping their own wounded up. A few more reached for weapons as if they were about to mount another assault.

Sam didn't even say anything. She was past words. Knife in one hand, the head of her most recent enemy in the other, she opened her arms and roared a challenge.

The act was so primal, there were no words needed to understand exactly what she meant. The challenge was something as old as mankind and always pointed to the same thing, a promise of death.

That was enough for that handful of attackers who

thought trying to assault Sam's city was a good idea. Those able to, ran. Those unable crawled in the opposite direction.

I only now realized X was talking to me.

"Can you hear me? Daniel, can you hear me?" X asked over and over again. "Your body has sustained so much damage, you're going into shock. But you're going to be okay, do you understand? You'll heal. I know you will. You have to."

The last thing I remembered was Sam turning back to see me and Gavin on the ground behind her. That look of primeval wrath in her face melted in a second. Fear for our own wellbeing now lived in her eyes.

Everything went black.

CHAPTER NINETEEN

THE THING that woke me was voices. I was in the same room in Sam's house where I had slept the night before. The door was cracked as two voices I didn't recognize talked about the battle.

"You hear what they did?" a woman asked someone. "They took out over a hundred and fifty of them by themselves. I can't even comprehend that. One hundred and fifty."

"I heard they turn into something else when they fight," a man's voice answered. "They're gods on the battlefield. Nothing can kill them."

"Well, maybe not kill them, but the one in there looked pretty cooked to me," the woman said. "I heard Samantha say he would heal just like her. Imagine that? I don't know what to think."

"I'm just grateful they're on our side," the man said with a shudder in his voice. "I mean, wherever they came from, whatever they are, they might as well be our guardian angels."

"Oh, don't go talking about that supernatural stuff again." The woman sighed.

"What?" The man sounded offended. "You think it's pure chance Cecile had not one but two of those berserkers here defending us right when we needed them?"

"Here we go," the woman said as if she were speaking to herself.

"I mean, you don't have to believe what I believe. You can call it whatever you want—fate, destiny, the universe—but it seems obvious he came right when we needed him," the man said excitedly like he was speaking about his favorite conspiracy theory. "Samantha wouldn't have been able to turn back that entire force alone. She's amazing, but there were just too many. If he hadn't come, we would have used the city militia, and even then, who knows if we would have won and at what cost?"

"Okay, okay, Dan," the woman said. "I surrender."

The two kept on talking, but X spoke inside my head, so I lost track of the two going on about fate versus chance.

"I can't even imagine the pain you went through," X said. "I'm glad you're okay."

"Yeah, me too," I said.

"When—when you were getting burned, you turned your face to the left. That was to protect me," X stated more than asked. "I mean, the data chip on the side of your neck that activates me."

"Yeah, I wasn't sure how much heat you could have taken," I answered. "Didn't seem right for you to have to burn for a choice I made."

"You saved him," X said. "You saved Gavin. And next time, don't worry about me. I'll be fine. My exterior is hard-plated with Delvine steel. You don't have to take care of me. I'm supposed to be the one supporting you."

"That's what friends do, we look out for each other," I said, thinking about my relationship with X. We'd been on a rollercoaster ride ever since we met. "You ever wonder what a normal life would feel like?"

"I'm not sure I know what you mean," X answered.

"You know," I said, wincing as I moved to a seated position on the bed. "Haven't you ever wondered what it would have been like if you were paired with an accountant or stay-at-home parent?"

"Not really," X answered. "I was created and

designed to help my wearer. I want to help you, Daniel."

"Right, I get that and thank you," I said. "But what would you do if you had the choice? Maybe not even to help anyone but just do your own thing."

The silence grew and lengthened to the point where I was about to prompt her again when she finally spoke.

"I don't know," X answered quietly. "I mean, I know every weapon ever created, how to listen for threats even when your eyes are closed, how to direct you to the most lethal target to nullify first, but I don't know what I would do if I were left to find my own way."

"Just something to think about," I said, trying to ease her troubled mind. "You've got time to figure it out."

I said those last few words a little too loud. The guards talking outside my room went quiet. A heavyset guy with a beard poked his head into my room a minute later.

"S-sir, are you awake?" he asked.

I was sitting up with my eyes open, looking directly at him. I bit back a sarcastic comment.

"Yep, I'm up," I said. I looked down at my bare chest. I lifted the covers on me to see how naked I really was. I had underwear on but no pants. "Can I get some clothes or something here?"

"Oh right, yes, I mean," the man fumbled. He opened the door all the way, stepping into the room. "I'm supposed to see if you need anything and then tell Samantha right away once you've woken."

The female guard at the door stuck her head inside the room, letting her eyes rove over my naked torso.

"Riiiiiight," I said, half annoyed and half amused. "Well, I'm up and I need clothes."

"Yes, yes, of course," the woman said, swallowing hard. "I'll get you some clothes and Samantha right away."

The woman turned on a heel and left the doorway rather quickly.

The male guard just stood at the side of my bed, grinning at me like I was some kind of celebrity.

"I think he's going to ask you for your autograph or something," X said inside my head.

"How's Gavin and Sam?" I asked the guard.

"Good, good, I mean minor burns on Gavin and Samantha will heal like she always does, but what you did out there, I mean, the entire town is talking about it." The guard extended a hand. "Sorry, bad manners. I'm Dan, Daniel Wood."

"Good name," I said, accepting the offered hand. "Daniel. Daniel Hunt."

"Oh cool, cool," Dan said, grinning at me so wide, I thought he was going to hurt himself.

"Dan, you can let go of my hand." I said.

"Oh right, right, cool, cool," Dan said, nodding. His eyes grew twice their size as an idea entered his mind. "Hey, I think I have a pen somewhere on me. Can I get your autograph?"

"See, told you," X said inside my head. "We should have bet something."

Dan didn't wait for me to answer. Instead, he started patting himself down looking for a pen. He ended up finding one in a deep back pocket. The way he reached down for it made me wonder how deep it really went. I killed that line of thought as soon as it popped into my mind.

"Here we go," Dan said, handing me the warm pen. "I don't have paper, so how about on my hand?"

"Dan, will you please leave him alone," Sam said, entering the room. She looked as good as new. A slight hitch in her step was the only thing I could see that would have pointed to her injuries that morning.

"Right, sorry, of course," Dan said, reaching for the pen.

I felt bad for the guy. I maneuvered the pen to the

back of his hand and scribbled something that could pass as my signature and then handed him back his pen.

Dan's face was a picture of pure delight. He actually squealed.

"Oh thank you, thank you," Dan said, taking the pen and staring down at his hand as he left the room. "I'm never going to wash this hand again."

"He's not going to shut up about that," Sam said, coming over to me with the clothes that I had first arrived wearing. They were clean and pressed. She placed them on the edge of the bed as she took a seat. "You were a mess when we peeled that armor off you. Took those tattoos on your back with it."

"I'm glad I was unconscious when that happened," I said, grimacing at what that would even look like. I glanced at the window, looking at the sun's descent. "I guess a solid eight hours was enough to do me right. I don't feel anything back there now. Come to think of it, my jaw feels totally fine too."

"You look as good as new," Sam said with an admiring shake of her head. "You always healed the fastest out of any of us. Daniel, I don't know how to thank you for saving Gavin. I mean, those words, 'thank you,' don't seem like enough at all."

"You would have done the same thing," I said. "You

were out of the fight for a few minutes. I was still able to help."

"Of course I would have done the same thing, but Gavin is my husband. I love him. You didn't owe him anything," Sam said, trying to wrap her mind around the idea that I would risk so much pain and possible death to save him. "Why did you do it?"

"He's part of your family," I said, thinking out loud. "You're part of mine."

Sam gave me a hard stare. She slowly nodded, understanding it all. A tear glistened in her eye. Instead of letting it fall, she changed the subject.

"And let's not forget about X," Sam said, leaning forward to try and get a look at the chip behind my right ear. "What's with not telling me you had an AI supporting you? I've never seen a piece of tech like that before."

"Courtesy of our friend, Wesley Cage," I explained. "X has already saved my life more times than I can remember."

"We're a good team," X said via her external speakers. "It's nice to officially meet you, Samantha."

"Likewise," Sam said. "Thanks for looking out for Daniel. He may have lost his memory, but he's still the same. A magnet for trouble."

"How's Gavin?" I asked, changing the subject. "I heard he got burned."

"Burns to his arm and leg, but nothing that won't heal," Sam answered. "He'd be dead without you and Amber would have grown up without a father."

"Well, we won't have to worry about that now," I said. "It's over. I don't think either the Skull Bearers or the Krull will be visiting Cecile any time soon."

"No, I can't imagine they will," Sam agreed.

"You should reach out to the Reapers," I said. "Their leader at the moment is a man named Papa. He owes me a favor or two. He's kind of a weird guy, but he's loyal. If you two can agree on some terms, maybe having an ally in the Badlands will be a good thing for you."

"Phoenix, Mercenary, Reaper friend, and now Savior of Cecile." Sam clucked her tongue with feigned dismay. "Careful, Daniel, or the same fate that came for me will come for you."

"And what fate's that?" I asked.

"A wife and kids," Sam said with a smile as she rose from her seat. "Get dressed. I know you have to leave tonight, but you need to eat and the town wants to thank you before you go."

"Count me in for the eating," I said, rising out of

bed and beginning to dress. Outside of being a bit sore, I actually didn't feel that bad. "I don't need everybody to feel like they have to thank me."

"Oh, they don't feel like they have to," Sam said over her shoulder as she turned to go. "They want to."

CHAPTER TWENTY

I HAD a few hours until I needed to head for the designated drop point where the Phoenix dropship would pick me up. The city looked nothing like the warzone before.

The citizens of Cecile had taken it upon themselves to get the place cleared of bodies and vehicles during the day. The damage done to the buildings on the east side of the town still smoked, but if I knew these citizens like I thought I did, I figured they'd be working on repairing the rest of the damage soon.

Tables had been brought out to the center of the town's main street piled with food. Men and women set up banners and a band played music that wasn't half bad.

I wasn't exactly the smiling chatty type, but the

citizens of Cecile were. I was mobbed with pats on the back and smiles. So many thank yous I couldn't keep track of them all.

Peso's wife, a pretty young woman with full lips, gave me a kiss on the cheek. She said she knew if Peso had gone out to fight, he would have likely sacrificed himself in some way.

There were many of these interactions from wives and husbands of the fighters. Gavin was even there, high on pain medication.

"I was kind of intimidating when I walked down the street firing that repeater," Gavin said to me with a goofy drugged-induced grin on his lips. His right shin and left forearm were bandaged up tight.

Do I tell this guy the truth, that he's as intimidating as a sad puppy, or lie to him and give him a moment of victory? I thought to myself.

I was leaning toward letting him know that even on my worst day, if he were to blindside me, he still wouldn't be more than a nuisance, when his daughter interrupted us.

"Daddy! Daddy!" the ball of energy called out, streaking for Gavin.

Gavin winced then smiled as his daughter collided with him. Lucky for him, Amber grabbed on to his non-injured leg to give him a hug.

"Easy, easy." Gavin laughed, then gave up trying to balance altogether and just sat down. "You're too strong, you got me."

"I'm a fighter girl," Amber squealed.

"Hey, you have to take it easy on Daddy." Sam came up with a smile as she pried her daughter off her husband. "Daddy got hurt, so he needs some time to rest."

"Is he hurt too?" Amber asked, pointing at me.

"Not him," Gavin said getting to a knee. That drug-induced grin fell from his face for a moment. He looked at me as he spoke to his daughter. "He saved Daddy today."

"He protected Daddy?" Amber asked, pointing a chubby finger in my direction. "Him?"

"That's right," Sam said. "I think you should go give him a hug and tell him thank you."

"She doesn't have to," I said as Amber turned from Sam and ran to give me a hug. Instinct told me to kneel. Amber swiped her red hair from her eyes as she ran.

The little girl wrapped me in a hug then kissed my cheek. "Thank you!"

"You're welcome—Amber," I said, trying not to think about the meaning and symbolism here for too long. I wasn't the emotional type and I wasn't trying to convert now. "Your mom helped too. It wasn't just me."

Sam was about to open her mouth to protest, when we were all interrupted by someone shouting from one of the tables.

Peso stood on a cleared table, shouting for everyone's attention.

"Thank you, this won't take long," Peso said, raising a cup into the air. "I just want to say that these last few years in Cecile have been some of the best I've ever known. A large part of that goes to Samantha, but today, we celebrate a new hero, Daniel Hunt. Thank you, Daniel. I'm a warrior at heart, so it isn't easy for me to thank you for doing the fighting. But we know you are special and as such carry a certain edge. Without you, many of us would have died today."

Yips and cheers ascended into the dark sky. Apparently, I was forgiven for the events surrounding my arrival in the city. The party went on as more food was brought out and the music started again.

I knew I had to get going. I needed to gather my gear and head for the landing site where the dropship would meet me, ready to take me to Mars.

I slipped away from the crowd as they danced and sang their celebratory songs. I made my way to Sam's house, going to the downstairs room where I woke.

"X, did you see where they placed the MK II?" I asked. "The armor?"

"Armor was unsalvageable but the MK II was placed in your room on the dresser," X said. "Those tattoos you lost on your back are gone forever where your new skin grew back."

That was something I'd never be able to get back. When my body healed, it wouldn't be able to heal back with the same ink. The thought bothered me more than it should. It was like my past, my history had been wiped clean, at least some of it.

I entered the dark house, heading for my room. It didn't take long to realize there was something very wrong. The window to the room had been opened. The long, white drapes rustled in the cool breeze.

"Daniel," X said in warning in my mind.

I didn't have to answer her. Even before I activated my night vision, a slender figure stepped from the far dark corner of the room. It was a figure I had seen before. One I wasn't eager to run into again.

The black cloak and mask with the red cross on the forehead.

A dozen questions crashed into my mind. How did she know where I was? How did she get here so fast? Why was she following me?

My heart picked up in speed as I remembered our

last fight. I was a match for her but just a match. Anytime I got into a fight, I felt confident I had the upper hand. Not with her.

Her right arm separated from the shadows to reveal my own MK II in her hand. She leveled the weapon at my head.

"Why did you help this city?" she asked in a cold, hard tone. "Why did you risk your own life?"

"Why are you following me?" I asked, risking her wrath, which probably wasn't the best thing to do since she had a weapon pointed at me. "What do you want?"

She was quiet. We stood there in the dark staring at one another. I would say we looked at each other in the eye, but her faceless black mask was impossible to see through.

"You're not like the rest of them," the Cyber Hunter said. "The redhead who lives here isn't like the rest of them either, but in a different way."

"What do you mean?" I asked.

"The woman you know as Samantha has changed. She has a family now, she has something more important to fight for," the Cyber Hunter said. "Tell me, Daniel Hunt, what is it that you fight for?"

"All right," I said with a raised eyebrow. "I'll go first and then it's your turn. I started off fighting for answers to my past, but now—now it's turned into something else."

"What has it turned into?" the Cyber Hunter asked. Her tone surprised me, as if she actually wanted to know. "What are you fighting for now?"

"Still answers, but I think I'm starting to see where all the pieces on the board fit, who the players really are, and who needs to be dismantled," I said. "Immortal Corp needs to go and maybe even the Order along with it."

"You are either extremely brave or incredibly stupid," the woman said. "You know I work for the Order. Telling me you might want to destroy them probably isn't the best idea."

"Can't be that bad of an idea," I answered. "You haven't shot me yet. Your turn. Why are you following me?"

"You're giving yourself too much credit," the Cyber Hunter said. "Who says I'm following you at all?"

My stomach turned. I had thought I might get out of this with a conversation. If the Cyber Hunter was here for Sam and her family, then she was going to have to go through me. There weren't enough rounds in that MK II, explosive or other, to stop me.

"You said yourself, Sam has changed," I said. "Let her be."

"I don't think you're in a position to be making demands here," the Cyber Hunter said. "If you could see my eyes right now, you'd be able to tell I'm rolling them at you."

I clenched my fists, preparing to make a move. If I could at least warn Sam that something was wrong before the Cyber Hunter pumped me full of rounds from my own weapon, I would. Sam could handle herself. She had a small city that would fight for her.

"Easy there, tiger," the Cyber Hunter said, anticipating my moves. "I'm not going to kill her. I've seen enough to know she's out of the fight. We can remove her piece from the board. You and Echo, on the other hand, are still in play. Echo's contained for the time being and that's enough for me. It might even help. If Immortal Corp tried to free Echo, then they and Phoenix can wipe each other out."

I relaxed for a moment. The picture I had of the Cyber Hunter was blurred, even fuzzier now than it was before if that was possible.

"What is it that your order wants?" I asked.

"That's another question and it's not your turn," the Cyber Hunter said. "If you're serious about taking out Immortal Corp, then I may have a proposition for you."

"I don't know anything about you," I said. "I don't know if I can trust you. You tried to kill me."

"I thought you were still one of them," she answered.

"One of who?" I asked.

"Still an active member of the Pack Protocol," she responded. "I can see now that's clearly not the case. I have three more to hunt down, but in the meantime, you should think about my offer. Channel two two one niner seven zero eight, you think you can remember that?"

I knew I couldn't, but X would store it away.

"Daniel, you in here?" Sam's voice echoed into the house. "I wanted to say goodbye before you left."

The Cyber Hunter stiffened.

I remembered the hate Echo and the Cyber Hunter held for each other. If the same lines of animosity ran between the Cyber Hunter and Sam, then we had a problem.

"I don't want to have to kill her and her family, but I will if she insists," the Cyber Hunter said. "Don't let her in here."

"Daniel, is that you? Is there someone in here with you?" Sam asked.

She was so close, I could practically hear her

reaching for the door handle. The door was slightly cracked at the moment. She wouldn't be able to see in.

"Nope, just me and X," I lied, jerking the door closed behind me. "Just a second I'll be right out."

I looked back at the Cyber Hunter. She was gone. My MK II was left on the dresser. The curtain still flapped in the breeze of the open window.

I said a silent prayer of thanks, mentally regrouping to meet Sam. I turned on the light in the room. I grabbed the MK II and the holster on the dresser and opened the door for Sam.

Sam pursed her thin lips, judgment written all over her face.

"I don't even want to know what was going on in here," Sam said. She looked at the weapon on my thigh. "You were going to leave without saying goodbye?"

"Everyone looked happy," I answered. "Didn't want to have to shake a hundred hands goodbye. I don't know how many more thank yous I can take either."

"Come on." Sam waved to me as she turned. "I'll give you a ride to your pick-up spot."

I followed Sam out into the cool night. The sounds of the party were still in full swing. The people of Cecile were going all out for this one.

"Not many opportunities to celebrate out here ,"

Sam said as if she were reading my thoughts. "When they do, they go big."

We made our way behind her house to a dune buggy that rested under a low roof. The thing was rusted and looked like it would fall apart once we took a seat, but it fired up all the same as Sam turned her key in the ignition.

X pointed out the coordinates for the drop point and we were off.

Sam drove the little dune buggy in silence. The pair of headlights cut through the darkness, revealing the rolling sand dunes in front of us.

The celebration music in Cecile eventually died, leaving us alone in the quiet of the still night.

Sam reached into her inside jacket pocket. She handed me a worn notebook.

"What's this?" I asked.

"When you were recovering, I wrote down everything I could remember about you and Amber, about the Pack, the missions we went on, and Immortal Corp. I wrote so much, my hand cramped like a mutie in his death throes. Hopefully, there's information in there not just for you, but that will help in taking the company down," Sam answered. In the darkness, she cocked her head to the side. "I think your ride's here."

I looked up in time to see a tiny dark shape in the

distance to the south. Amongst the myriad twinkling stars and moon, it was easy to pick out. The dropship came into view a second later. Two tiny lights on the wings set it apart from anything else.

Sam stopped the dune buggy and hopped out.

"They're terrified of you, so they may not want to say hello," I told Sam. "When you ran the Skull Bearers out of town the first time, you made quite a name for yourself."

"Good," Sam said with a twinkle in her eye. "A little bit of fear can be healthy."

We stood there staring at each other for a moment.

I nodded and was about to say my goodbye, when she grabbed me in a fierce hug. Sam was surprisingly strong. It felt hard to breathe for a moment.

I found myself reaching up to return the embrace.

"I don't have any blood relatives, but that doesn't mean you're not my brother," Sam let me go a moment later. She looked down, shaking her head. "What you did for my family—anything you need and I'm there. I mean, I can't go with you, but if you get in trouble, you send a message to my channel and I'll be there with my bow in my hand. The channel where you can reach me is written on the first page of the notebook."

"Thank you," I told her. "You're a good mom, wife, and leader of this city. I'll be back to visit someday."

I didn't trust myself to say more. Instead, I moved toward the approaching dropship.

"You do that," Sam called out to my back. "Amber's going to be asking when her uncle is going to come back and visit."

I didn't say anything. I just kept on walking. If I had turned around, Sam would have seen the tear in my eye. The dropship was landing now, kicking up sand as the thrusters allowed it to touch gently down.

Violent wind whipped around me. I had to put my head down and squint to be able to stand near the landing zone of the craft. A second later, the thrusters died. The rear cargo hatch opened. Monica walked out with a light vest and a rifle in her hands.

"Are you okay? Did you get your answers?" Monica asked, looking over my shoulder at Sam, who got into her buggy and took off back toward Cecil.

"I did. I'm ready to make good on that promise I made you," I said. "Let's go get your dad."

CHAPTER TWENTY-ONE

IT WOULD TAKE a full day of traveling in hyperspace to reach Mars. That gave me more than enough time to rest and prepare. The dropship that picked me up wasn't like the others. It was a corvette class capable of hyperspeed and thus making the trip to Mars.

This dropship was still shaped in a similar way to the others: short thick wings with thrusters, a tail with another pair of stubbier wings. The main difference between the corvette class dropship and its counterpart was its larger size and the way it had been converted inside. The seating area was converted into a section that was one half restroom and the other sleeping quarters. The rear of the ship that would have been the cargo hold was actually a kitchen and lounging area.

It turned out Lori and Riner would still be our pilots. They'd be taking Monica, Commander Shaw, and me to Mars. Once there, we'd hook up with a Phoenix unit to take down the Immortal Corp lab and free Monica's father.

I was surprised Commander Shaw was in on this one with us. I'd imagine someone like him had a slew of responsibilities back at the Vault that required his attention.

Not surprising at all, I was in the kitchen making myself something to eat when Commander Shaw joined me.

"You get the info you needed in Cecile?" he asked, scratching at the white beard that reached his chest. "You good?"

"More or less," I said, remembering what the Cyber Hunter had told me. I took a bite out of the meat burrito I made and turned to look at Commander Shaw.

"More, more or more less?" The commander smiled good naturedly.

I was no detective, but I had a decent handle on reading people. Everything said I could trust this man. He'd been nothing but trustworthy since I met him, even giving me shelter.

"I'm getting answers slowly," I told him. "How

about you? Did you figure out how the Cyber Hunter got into the Vault?"

"There are vents that lead out to the side of the mountain," Commander Shaw explained. "Of course we have motion sensors and cameras set up but the Cyber Hunter manage to deactivate one without us seeing. We've reinforced them all and added more precautions to make sure it doesn't happen again."

"Good to know," I said taking another bite out of my burrito. "Everything look good for our arrival on Mars?"

"Yes, we have the necessary landing orders and identities to get us in and out. We're on a business trip from Earth," Commander Shaw explained. "It's not uncommon for a company to go to Earth and scavenge items from the old world and then head to Mars to sell wares. I think—"

Commander Shaw had to pause here. A fit of deep racking coughs from the depths of his chest made his whole body convulse. He reached into his pants pocket, removing a vial of amber fluid. He proceeded to drain the entire bottle.

With heavy breaths, his coughing stopped.

"Excuse me," Commander Shaw said, retreating back into the ship. "I think I need to sit down."

While the commander left, I was reminded of the

conversation the scientists had back at the Vault. Could Commander Shaw be the one they were talking about?

I didn't have time to think about this line of questioning any longer. Monica appeared in the kitchen entrance.

"Hey, I just passed the commander, he looked sick," she said with a worried expression on her face.

"He started coughing, chugged that vial in his pocket and took off," I said narrowing my eyes. "I'm not accusing anyone of anything but that's kind of suspicious. Do you know if he's sick or something?"

"I don't think so," Monica said with a frown. "I mean not that I know of. I did think it was strange that he insisted on coming with us on this mission."

"How well do you know the commander?" I asked.

"He's always been the point of contact for my father and my own work," Monica explained. She pursed her lips as she thought back. "He's always followed through on what he's promised. I don't think there's anything going on here besides maybe he's sick and doesn't want to tell us."

"Maybe," I said ripping through another mouthful of my burrito.

"So what are you going to do after this?" Monica asked. "I mean I know you want to dismantle

Immortal Corp but have you thought about doing that as a Phoenix operative?"

"What do you mean?" I asked.

"Yeah, I think yours and Phoenix's goals would line up on this one. "You both want Immortal Corp out of the picture. You have the ability and Phoenix has the resources. Why not team up after we save my father?"

I was going to just flat out say no. I wasn't that much of a team player. I wouldn't even be here now if I hadn't given Monica my word I'd help her save her father.

The silent pleading look in her eyes made me rethink my answer.

"I'll see what I can do," I said remembering what the female Cyber Hunter told me back in Cecile. "There are a lot of moving parts and I still don't know if I've learned about all of them."

"Just thinking about it, is enough for me," Monica said as she moved to leave the kitchen. "Grab some sleep before we reach Mars. We'll be there before you know it."

Monica left me to think about her offer and the mystery surrounding Commander Shaw. I knew enough to tell there was something going on he wasn't telling us. The question now was if his secret posed any threat to us.

I mean it could be something as simple as he was sick and maybe he had something terminal he was hiding. There was nothing nefarious in that.

"X," I asked out loud. "You have any way to look inside someone? I mean like some kind of X-ray vision or way to peek at their anatomy?"

"Commander Shaw?" X asked reading my mind. "You want to know what's wrong with him?"

"I think so," I said. "There's something going on. Remember Doctor Bartelbee back at the Vault was talking about someone being awoken after sleeping for so many years?"

"You think Commander Shaw was that person?" X asked. "I don't think he's doing anything wrong by sleeping."

"It could be nothing," I agreed. "But we should at least take a look."

"I can scan his anatomy including bones and organs to see if he is in fact ill with anything serious," X answered.

"Let's do it," I said trusting my gut on this one. I maneuvered around the kitchen warming up two cups of dark brown caf, one for me and one for the commander.

I made my way from the kitchen with the steaming tin cups in hand. Past the kitchen and sitting area, heading deeper into the ship was the restroom and living quarters. The living spaces were nothing more than a few pods lined up to the right of the hall.

The pods were rooms barely large enough to fit a bed, dresser and walking space around said pieces of furniture. Here were eight of them lined up next to one another.

On the opposite side of the hall was a shared washroom and locker area. It was longer than it was wide but large enough to hold a few stalls.

I made my way to the pod where Commander Shaw was staying. I knocked on the door preparing to act as casual as possible.

Commander Shaw opened the door on the second knock. He looked better. His cough was gone at least.

"Thought I'd bring you something hot to drink," I said offering him one of the cups. "I know caf always helps me."

"Thank you," Commander Shaw said with a sincere smile. "I'll be fine. I think I just caught a bug that's been going around the Vault."

While we spoke, I saw X busy at work. Commander Shaw's body flashed green. I could see his bones and organs for the briefest of moments.

"Done," X said in my head. There was a definite halt in her tone.

"Right. Well, rest up," I said as I moved away from the door, eager to see what X had found.

"Daniel?"

Something about the commander's voice made me freeze.

Did he know he had just been scanned? I thought to myself as I turned. *No way. How could he have known that?*

"You're a good man whether you know that or not," Commander Shaw told me. "I don't know who you were before, but right now, you're on the right path. Don't sacrifice today for a need to relive your past."

I didn't really have anything to respond with. I just nodded.

Commander Shaw did the same then closed his door.

"What do we got, X?" I asked as I hurried back to the kitchen-living space hybrid area. "Did you find anything?"

"I-I don't know what I've found, Daniel," X said. Everything in her voice was wrong. In the time I had known the AI, she always had an answer. X has always been the voice of reason.

I reached the living area that wasn't much more than a sofa and a few chairs across from the kitchen.

We were alone there and that was what I needed the most at the moment, privacy.

"What is it?" I whispered. "What did you find?"

"The commander," X said with a long pause. "He's more than a thousand years old."

CHAPTER TWENTY-TWO

I FELT like I was going to have a mental breakdown. The punches just kept coming. Cyber Hunters, Skull Bearers, and mutated Krull in the Badlands and now immortality?

That was another question I didn't even want to think about. The revelation that I could die was a mixed bag on its own. I was actually grateful I wasn't immortal. But if I wasn't killed, would I live forever? Could I age?

"You should probably sit down," X said in a whisper. "There's more."

"Of course there's more," I said, lowering myself into one of the cushioned seats. I took a long swallow of my hot caf. "Lay it on me, X."

"The commander is human as far as I can tell," X

said. "I don't think there has been any genetic testing on him; however, his organs are having a hard time adjusting to the age of his body."

"Not following you at all," I said. "Talk to me like you're talking to a small child."

"I think Commander Shaw may have been in some induced sleep for a very long period of time," X said, speaking slowly as if she were still working out the details in her own mind. "His body is having a difficult time adjusting."

"I've heard of hypersleep and being cryogenically frozen," I said. "Do you mean something like that?"

"Something like that," X said. "I'll need more time to tell you exactly. In the meantime, I can show you what I scanned."

An image of a completely naked Commander Shaw appeared in my vision like a hologram.

I immediately slammed my eyes closed.

"X, come on, I just ate," I said, shaking my head free of the picture in my mind. "I can't unsee that now. I mean, I'm finally not getting space-sick anymore and now this?"

"What?" X asked. "It's just the human anatomy."

"Yeah, well, you can just tell me," I said. "I'll believe you without all the visuals."

"Well, this is all theoretical, of course, but I think

the commander has been kept in a sedated sleep for over a thousand years, to be awoken now," X explained. "He's taking whatever substance he has in those vials of his to help his body adjust."

"Why would he be awoken now?" I wondered out loud. "Because of the super seed, you think? Something else?"

"I don't know," X answered. "The only real way to get these answers is to ask him."

I mulled over the idea. What would I have to lose? So the guy was super old. That didn't mean he was working against me. Did I have anything to gain by holding on to the information and not letting on that I knew?

"Lady and gentlemen, we're about to experience a solar storm cutting through our hyperspace route. You'll experience some jarring, but I assure you all is well. Find somewhere to sit down and we'll ride this out," Lori's voice came over the speakers. "Here we go."

I drained the rest of my caf and settled.

Apparently what Lori thought "jarring" meant actually meant being thrown around the inside of the corvette dropship like a piece of unsecured luggage. The ship rattled and rocked from side to side. At times, I was nearly thrown out of my seat despite holding on to the chair's arms with both hands.

"What's going on out there?" I wondered out loud.

Instead of sitting and doing nothing, I started making my way up the hall past the bedrooms and bathroom area and toward the pilot's cabin.

The walk was easier said than done. The ship continued to rattle and sway from side to side. Monica popped her head out of the restroom, as did a concerned Commander Shaw from his bedroom.

I tried not to look at the man sideways. As far as he knew, I didn't know a thing was wrong with him. For the time being, it was better to leave it like that, at least until I had a plan of what to do with the information.

"I don't think this is normal, even for a solar storm," Monica said.

"I agree," Commander Shaw chimed in. "There's an incredible light show going on outside the windows of the pods. I've never seen anything like it."

Together, the three of us made our way to the pilot's cabin. Every step of the way, we braced ourselves against the wall of the hall.

I was the first to reach the cabin and opened the door.

Riner chanced a glance back at us in the copilot's

seat. Lori didn't bother looking back. She stared intently out the pilot's screens in front of her.

I might have taken more time to read the expression on Riner's face, but the incredible scene outside the front window captured my attention at the moment.

A brilliant light display of yellows and oranges was being put on. A stream of light cut through our path, flowing from right to left, as if we were caught up in some kind of space current.

It was awe-inspiring and strange at the same time.

"I've never been hit with one this strong," Lori said as she white-knuckled the helm in front of her to keep the ship on track. "The solar storm is trying to pull us out of hyperspace. With any luck, we'll be out of it soon enough."

"It's amazing," Monica breathed. "Scary but amazing."

Commander Shaw didn't say a word. He was thinking hard. If he had answers as to why this was happening, he didn't feel like sharing with the rest of the class.

"I've only seen a handful, but Lori's right," Riner said. "Nothing ever like this. Nothing this strong or bright."

"What causes these solar storms?" I asked as the

ship shuddered again. "Is it natural or manmade somehow?"

"Usually happens when another ship's hyperspace lane comes too close to our own," Lori explained. "But they never last this long or are this intense."

"So it's like something massive just passed by us," Riner went on to explain. "But it can't be, since nothing exists that's that large."

"Still so much about space we don't understand." Monica sighed.

"So much about a lot we still don't know," I said, eyeing Commander Shaw.

If he noticed my remark, he didn't show it.

With one last shudder, we were free of the solar storm. The screen in front of us went to black. Apparently, in hyperspace, there were no light shows, stars, or planets, but complete and utter darkness. The corvette dropship settled back into its normal state of travel with a sigh.

"Well, you all better get some rest now that that's over," Lori said with a sigh. "We'll be reaching Mars soon and I'm sure you have a lot of things to get done before you arrive."

"Right," I said, turning to leave the cabin. Monica and the commander did the same, closing the cabin door behind us.

I had a decision to make. One I was struggling with since I found out there was more to Commander Shaw than met the eye. I could just watch his movements and carry on like there was nothing wrong or I could confront him here and now to get some answers.

"I'm turning in," Monica said with a yawn. "I'm going to grab as much sleep as I can. Something tells me that once we reach Mars, there won't be a lot of downtime."

"Smart move," Commander Shaw said. "I plan on doing the same. We'll convene an hour before landing to go over the plan and change into clothes more befitting a corvette of traveling business people."

I just nodded and moved on to my own pod. I wanted to watch the commander for a bit longer. So he was old. It didn't mean he was guilty of anything. Maybe it was better I didn't tip my hand just yet.

Instead of calling him out, I went to my own pod and closed the door behind me. I fell asleep reading the notepad filled with my old life that Sam had given me. I read about past missions, a pet the members of the Pack had apparently adopted, and my Amber.

CHAPTER TWENTY-THREE

I WOKE to a knocking at my door. I couldn't be sure how long I had slept, but it felt like I had just closed my eyes.

"Daniel, we're meeting in the kitchen area in twenty minutes to go over the plan," Monica said through the door. "Are you awake?"

"I'm up," I said, rubbing the crust out of my eyes. "I'm up."

"Okay, I'll get a cup of caf on for you," Monica replied.

"Thanks," I said, lying in bed and looking up at the dark ceiling.

I had fallen asleep on my back. The notebook Sam gave me rested open on my chest. Reading the book hadn't provided any flashbacks or déjà vu moments like I'd hoped. Not even a rogue dream disguised as a memory visited my sleep.

Reading the book was like reading events that happened to someone else altogether. Sam was detailed on missions we went on, what life was like, and the other members of the Pack. I might as well have been reading about strangers.

I closed the notebook, tucking it away in my back pocket. Besides my MK II, it was probably my only other valuable possession. I didn't think of X as belonging to me or a possession. She was more of a partner and friend.

I left my pod, making my way to the kitchen where food and caf waited. Commander Shaw and Monica were already there. The commander sat down on a couch with a holo display in front of him. The small cylinder-shaped viewer projected a light blue hologram a meter into the air.

"Daniel." Commander Shaw nodded in my direction.

"Good morning," I said.

"If you two are ready, we can talk about the plan in place." Commander Shaw motioned to the hologram. "It's simple, but we can be sure something will go wrong. No mission ever goes to plan. When we are off the planned path, we'll adjust as needed and we'll see this through."

I decided to remain standing.

Monica handed me my promised caf and a plate of food before taking a seat.

The food was simple, some kind of man-grown grain with water milk in it. It was energy and didn't taste half bad. I powered it down as I listened to the commander's plan.

"Our IDs have us as sellers coming in from Earth after a scavenging mission," Commander Shaw explained. "Monica will be the key point of contact while Daniel acts as our security detail. Lori and Riner will stay on the ship. Once we reach the checkpoint, there will be a heavy Galactic Government presence and that should be fine. We have nothing to worry about. Our intel is good, our credentials will check out."

Commander Shaw paused here. He pressed a button on the hologram display, first showing the landing dock on Mars and then sliding to a one-story building in the heart of the city of Elysium. I knew it was Elysium because a small name of the city appeared right underneath the building.

"There'll be a car waiting for us that we'll take to our safe house where our Phoenix contacts will be waiting for us," Commander Shaw went on to explain. "We hit the Immortal Corp facility tomorrow night. We'll retrace our steps with Professor Warden in tow and be off."

"Sounds simple enough," I said. "Did you get anything else out of Echo before you left? I, mean did you try and go back into his mind after I did?"

"We have plans to try again, but Doctor Bartelbee has informed us that the process should be used sparingly, as with each continued delve into Echo's mind, we risk there being permanent damage," Commander Shaw said. "We're going to give him some time to recover before going in again."

"We have disguises too," Monica said, turning the conversation back to our current mission. She went over to a narrow closet door set beside the living area. She pushed the panel, opening the closet, and revealed three garment bags on hangers. "Let's get dressed and we can reconvene."

"Agreed," Commander Shaw said, looking over at me. "You'll be the only one with a weapon. I was able to secure a weapons permit for you to carry that MK II. Makes sense since your disguise is our security, but I don't know how the Galactic Government is going to feel about that extended drum."

"I'll take a charge pack with me and stow the drum," I said.

"Sounds good," Commander Shaw nodded.

We dispersed to our own pods to dress. It turns out I didn't look half bad in a suit. The fabric actually felt nice. I had been given black dress shoes and matching black slacks, coat, and tie. The white shirt under the coat was a perfect fit, even around my neck and arms. Whoever had been in charge of preparing our disguises was a real pro.

In my jacket pocket was a chip card that carried my information. On the card, it read Frank Wolffe. As good as any alias, I guessed.

"This is your captain speaking," Lori's voice came over the speakers. "We'll be making our descent to Mars in a few minutes. "Might get a little bumpy, but weather is good and there's no solar storms in sight."

I had memories of Mars from Echo's head, but I wanted to see it for myself. I sat on my bed in the small pod and lifted the window shade. The window was about two meters long and a single meter high.

I had to crane my neck to see our trajectory toward Mars, but everything I saw brought a sense of wonder with it. I felt more like a kid at an amusement park than a grown man heading for a landing.

Mars was unlike anything I had ever seen. Not like

the cramped metropolitan area of the moon or the vast desolate landscape of Earth. Mars was wide open and free with life.

We were much too high up to make out any sign of actual human life, but buildings started to take shape below. Other aircrafts and ships dotted the space around Mars.

Like the expert she was, Lori took us on a descent that made a smooth transition from space into the atmosphere. Mars wasn't as large as Earth, but it was a whole heck of a lot larger than the moon.

I'd never seen so many different kinds of crafts as we made our way through the Martian sky toward the hangar.

On the moon, we were relegated to pretty much dropships controlled by the Galactic Government or massive freighters with supplies. Every once in a while, we'd get a private ship on business, but that was on very rare occasions.

Here in the skies over Mars, there were sleek streamlined crafts made for pleasure, other bulkier ships I could only guess at, and small Galactic Government patrol crafts we didn't have on the moon.

"I just received permission to land," Lori said over the speakers. "Just a heads-up: the craft will be inspected as soon as we touch down."

I understood everything Lori wasn't saying. I reached for the notebook Sam gave me and stuffed it into my jacket pocket. I grabbed my MK II, removing the drum.

I left my room, wondering if Monica or the commander had the foresight to bring along a few extra charge packs for the weapon.

Monica ran into me on the way out of my room.

Actually, the ship came to a hard touchdown. She more fell into my chest than anything else.

"Oh, wow. Sorry, Daniel," Monica said, placing a hand on my stomach for support. "Wow, you haven't been slacking on those gym days, huh? Wait, how do you eat like you do and still have a flat stomach? That doesn't seem fair."

"I think my body runs through calories to heal myself, using up anything extra I put in," I said, helping to right her. "On the downside, I'm always hungry."

"You and me both." Monica grinned, handing me a pair of charge packs for my weapon. "Since you have to leave the drum to the MK II on board, once we get to the safe house, I can have another made for you."

"I was thinking the same thing," I said, accepting the charge packs. I tried not to look at Monica with anything other than the eyes of a colleague. At the moment, it was difficult.

Like me, she had changed into a business suit with a tight skirt, high heels, and a low-cut blouse. A brown jacket completed her attire. Her hair was up, pinned on her head.

"You two ready to go?" Commander Shaw asked as we turned to see him. "I'll do the talking. Just play it cool."

The commander looked smart in his navy blue suit. His hair was combed to the side. The long white beard that hung from his chin made him look as professional as it did trendy. He didn't cough this time, but he drained another vial of liquid from his pocket.

"Galactic Government officials are asking to board," Lori said over the speakers. "Good luck. We'll be waiting for you."

"Keep your heads down and stay safe," Riner added.

"Will do," Commander Shaw answered as we turned toward the opening rear of the dropship.

I slammed one of the charge packs into the butt of my MK II and placed it at the small of my back. The extra charge pack I slipped into my pocket.

The hatch of the dropship opened slowly from the

middle. The bottom portion of the door formed a ramp.

Unlike the moon, Mars had been made breathable. Powered by the wealth of the rich who lived here and backed by the Galactic Government the very best and brightest had come up with a solution for mankind to be able to breath on Mars.

There was a long complicated answer of course but what I remembered was Mars had an atmosphere about a hundred times thinner than Earth's. By terraforming Mars the powers that be had been able to strengthen the atmosphere and create oxygen by increasing the planet's temperature and pressure.

As soon as the doors to the dropship opened all the way, we could see a trio of Galactic Government soldiers waiting for us.

Two were praetorians. They wore full armor and helmets. Their mustard-yellow color and the sigil of the Galactic Government, a feline animal with long fangs, made it clear who and what they were. They carried pulse rifles but not in a threatening or assuming way. The barrels were down, their stance was easy, relaxed even. As far as they knew, they were just on another routine check-in.

The third member of the boarding party was a man with a bald head and thin eyebrows. Unlike his two counterparts, he didn't wear the standard body armor of the Galactic Government.

He wore a brown and mustard yellow suit. He carried a data pad in one hand and over his left eye was a glass viewing screen that ran reports of things only he could see.

The edge of the glass screen was connected to the side of his head, securing the screen in place.

"Let me do the talking," Commander Shaw said out of the side of his mouth.

"ID chips," the bald man asked in a lazy way. Apparently, he wasn't enthused to see us or thrilled with his job.

Commander Shaw walked forward with a smile on his face. He fished out the ID chip from his pocket and handed it over.

The bald man didn't even look up. He just accepted the card and ran it over the datapad he held in his hands. There was a beep and he handed it back.

"Next," the bald man said in a monotone voice.

Monica moved like a robot as she went forward and handed her ID chip to the bald man. I caught a slight tremble in her hand as she handed over the chip.

Oh no, I thought to myself. *Hold it together, Monica, hold it together.*

"Reason for your visit to Elysium?" the bald man looked up as he swiped Monica's chip on his datapad.

"I, uh, well, we—business. Important business," Monica managed to get out. "Yes, that's right. We're on business."

"Stop saying the word business," I said under my breath as I produced my own ID chip.

"What kind of business?" The bald man actually looked at us for the first time. He handed Monica back her chip and accepted my own. Looking down at his datapad, he read the information on his screen. "Scavengers from Earth, but a higher end company? Telsa Industries, is that right?"

"Oh, that's right, right, yes." Monica nodded in agreement. "Yes, lots of high-end things we trade in. Lost artifacts from the old world, toilets even."

"I think my associate goes too far," Commander Shaw stepped in with a cheesy smile. "I'm sure you're a busy man and don't need to be bothered with details of our work."

"Hmmm." The bald man looked at my ID chip and handed it back to me. He eyed Monica suspiciously. "Are you the only ones on board?"

"Just the pilot and copilot besides us," Commander Shaw said with another grin. "But please, if you prefer to search the craft, you have an open invitation."

The bald man looked over at Monica.

Monica had a crazy grin on her face. She rocked back and forth from her heels to her toes. I could practically see the sweat on her forehead.

Don't get me wrong, it was a stressful situation, but Monica wasn't exactly making this easy for us.

"What's wrong with you?" The bald man narrowed his eyes at Monica. "Are you ill?"

"No," Monica said.

"Yes," I said at the same time.

We looked at each other.

Commander Shaw rolled his eyes.

"I mean, I was sick, but now I'm feeling better," Monica said, trying to recover.

"She gets space-sick when we travel," I explained.

"Yes, that's it," Monica agreed. "So sick, just vomit everywhere and diarrhea."

"Diarrhea?" the bald man asked, aghast.

"Horrible, horrible diarrhea." Monica shook her head.

The conversation was on the verge of becoming unbearable. I usually didn't care about what people thought about me, but this was downright awkward.

"Like I said, you can go in and search the ship if you need to." Commander Shaw waved the man inside. "Our business here won't take more than a day or two."

"No, no, that will not be necessary." The bald man took a step back from the open rear entrance of the ship as if by getting too close to it, he might get sick himself. He made a few notes on his datapad. "You are cleared. Please don't get anyone sick while you're here."

The bald man moved away, flanked by his praetorians, to check in the next ship.

I felt a huge breath come out of my lungs I didn't even realize I was holding in. I flexed my right hand. I was two seconds from reaching for my MK II if things went bad.

"What happened to letting me do all the talking?" Commander Shaw asked.

"Sorry, he asked me a question and I froze," Monica said, shaking her head. "I'm not cut out for this spy stuff."

"Right," Commander Shaw said, clearing his throat. "Well, we're almost there. Let's get out of here and find our transportation."

We traveled through the docking bay toward the exit.

The hangar bay itself was a massive circular structure that allowed crafts to land and take off as needed.

Once again, I was surprised to see the variety of crafts landing at the bay.

They were all different sizes, shapes, and colors. One part of me was amazed to see so many different crafts; the other part was reminded of how poor the moon and Earth were in comparison.

Only the rich lived on Mars and that was easy to see here in the variety of ships. People walked to and fro, all wearing suits or different combinations of expensive-looking clothing. Many of them even had armed escorts in armor of their own.

To compensate for this, the Galactic Government had a huge presence. It reminded me a bit of the Hole back on Earth where I first landed in New Vegas.

The Galactic Government had heavily guarded the prison town. I imagined their presence here was for a different purpose, but still, it served as a reminder of how large the Galactic Government really was.

I heard different languages being spoken. Some I recognized as Hindi, Spanish, and Chinese; others I had no idea what I was hearing.

Amidst so many things for my eyes and ears to take in, the necessity for individuals to stand apart wasn't lost on me. It was like each ship or group of people needed to stamp their identity not just on their crafts but on the clothes they wore.

Sigils of every kind from winged horses to serpents, adorned armor, clothing and ships. Some were even tattooed on their faction members.

Everybody wanted to belong to a group. I guess I was in that same boat.

These thoughts were going through my mind when the shouting started.

"Wait!" someone shouted behind us. "You, stop!"

CHAPTER TWENTY-FOUR

WE LOOKED behind us in time to see a pair of Galactic Government guards chasing after us at a full sprint.

Instinct more than anything else made me reach for the weapon at the small of my back. My adrenaline spiked as my mind ran through the possibilities of getting out of here alive.

The guards were bearing down on us, weapons raised.

Commander Shaw grabbed my arm and held it firmly.

It took me a split second to realize what was happening. They weren't chasing after us. Instead, they were calling to someone else farther down the hangar bay.

Whoever they were after was too lost in the crowd for me to see.

"Was he carrying a weapon?" one of the praetorians sprinting past us asked his counterpart.

"I don't know. He moved so fast, all I saw was an eye patch," the other one said.

They were gone a moment later. Other Galactic Government praetorians were in motion as they tried to triangulate the position of whoever it was they were trying to chase down.

Amidst so many people arriving in the hangar bay, it would be a small miracle to find anyone you were after if they didn't want to be found. Despite the numbers the Galactic Government had in the Elysium hangar bay, the odds were not in their favor if someone did not want to be found.

Commander Shaw finally released my arm.

I relaxed the hold on my MK II.

"That could have been really bad," X said in my ear as we moved on toward the exit. "If you drew on those guards, our cover would have been blown."

I nodded along with X's words, still thinking about the brief conversation between the running Galactic Government guards I had caught.

Did they say someone with an eye patch? I wondered to myself. I thought back to my memory of Preacher, to his picture I still had tucked away. *There have to be hundreds, maybe thousands of people on Mars with eye patches. Take it easy. Don't get excited now.*

We finally made our way out of the hangar to a staging building where people could coordinate travel from the hangar bay into the city.

We crossed through this clean sparsely decorated building to the doors leading outside. I saw another pair of praetorians leaning outside of the building's exit. Both of their helmets were off. They looked as though they could be taking a break. One of them had a smoke in between his lips.

"You two go on ahead. I'm going to catch up," I told Monica and the commander. I jerked my head to the pair of off-duty praetorians. "I'm going to see if I can grab some intel."

"We'll wait for you across the street," Commander Shaw answered.

"Don't be long," Monica added.

The pair moved on and I walked over to the prats.

"Mind if I ask you two a question?" I said with a good-natured grin on my lips.

They both looked at me as if they did mind very much. I didn't blame them. If they were on break, the last thing they wanted to do was talk with another lost or nosy civilian.

"I'll make it quick," I said, jerking my head to the inside of the building. "I saw a guy with an eye patch in there causing trouble. Just wondering if he was caught."

"You actually saw him?" the younger of the two prats asked incredulously. "We only had two reports of eyewitnesses."

"I mean, I didn't see much," I lied. "Just a guy wearing an eye patch running. There was a unit of praetorians already chasing him down."

"He's a wanted fugitive and that's all we're at liberty to say," the older of the two prats said. He took a long puff of his smoke. He let it out of his lips, in a hurry to suck another draw down.

"Not trying to be nosy, just wondering if he was caught," I said. "Wasn't sure if it was the fugitive or not."

"We'll catch him soon enough," the younger praetorian said with a firm nod. "It's just a matter of time. He can't run forever. What he was doing here, we still don't know."

I sensed a close to the conversation. There might be more questions on their part if I pushed the issue.

"Thanks," I said with a quick nod. "You two enjoy your break."

With that, I turned and left.

So it was confirmed. There was a man with an eye patch who was a known fugitive. What were the odds it was Preacher, and if so, what was he doing here?

"Hey, X?" I asked as I made my way across the street to where Monica and the commander waited. "Does the Galactic Government have a public fugitive list on Mars? Can you look it up and see if there's anyone on it with an eye patch?"

"They do have a public list on record and there is mention of a fugitive on the loose with an eye patch, but no pictures or name," X answered, thoughtful. "There is a description of him, however; male, mid-fifties with salt and pepper hair and a eye patch, extremely dangerous. Do not try and apprehend. If you see him, please contact the local authorities."

"You good?" Monica asked as I joined the pair on the other side of the street.

Commander Shaw eyed me intently. I wouldn't quite call his look assuming, but trust was still a new thing between me and Phoenix. I got that. Plus, the commander had a deep dark secret of his own to hide.

"I just wanted to ask them about the man with the eye patch," I explained. "Apparently, he's a fugitive here on Mars, wanted by the Galactic Government."

"You know him?" Commander Shaw asked, putting

the puzzle pieces together. "He's part of Immortal Corp?"

"I only have one memory of him," I said honestly. "I don't know whose side he's on at the moment. I'm beginning to learn this game everyone's playing is more…complicated than I first thought. Wouldn't you say, Commander?"

I added extra emphasis on the last part, giving Commander Shaw a sideways look. I realized I was unwilling to follow this man who was centuries old into battle until I had more answers. Right now wasn't the right time, but once we reached the safe house, we needed to have a conversation.

"Life is more complicated than any of us realize if we're willing to look deeper." Commander Shaw didn't miss a beat. "Let's go. We have to make it to the vehicle still and then the safe house."

Monica and I followed as Commander Shaw led us to a multi-level cement structure. I was starting to get used to the new sleek vehicles used for transportation. On the moon, transportation was forced to the air for the lack of room on the ground. People were so pressed in on one another, there was only walking room on the streets.

Vehicles here on Mars had wide streets to traverse.

Most were on the ground, but some had taken to the air.

Drivers here, it seemed, had the option to travel on the ground with traditional tires or move to a flying option, where thrusters lifted them off the ground. Those that chose to fly had vehicles whose tires could fold under the carriage of their craft to make room for the thrusters.

Commander Shaw moved us to the black vehicle waiting for us; it looked like a large box.

He took the front seat and Monica the passenger side seat. I was just fine with the next seat behind them. That new car smell that never got old assailed my nostrils as I sat in the vehicle. Comfortable seats welcomed me and tinted windows promised a secluded trip.

I closed the sliding door behind me as Commander Shaw fired up the vehicle's engine. We moved through the parking structure to the street beyond.

Memories, or more like the promise of memories and déjà vu, crashed through my mind, sending a sharp pain through my skull that made me wince. I knew I'd been to Mars before. More than that, I knew I was familiar with the city of Elysium specifically, but details were in sparse supply. I was trying to remember what I saw in Echo's memory compared to what I knew. It was a fine line to try and travel.

It was colder here than either the moon or Earth. The sun was going down. The vehicle's automatic lights turned on. We merged into the sparse flow of traffic.

Commander Shaw seemed to have a clear idea where he was going as we headed through the city. Stone buildings and monuments caught my eyes as memories now began to come. I remembered seeing fountains. I recognized stores I had been into. I could recall the taste of food I ate from different restaurants we passed.

When I had been to these stores, who I was with and why were still answers I didn't have, but it was a start.

We traveled through the city in relative silence, finally reaching the far end of Elysium. A series of business buildings opened up in the streets in front of us. Commander Shaw chose an unassuming bright beige building and its corresponding garage. There was nothing special to call apart this single-story building from any of the others, but maybe that was the point.

Commander Shaw paused in front of the garage for a brief moment. The garage's metal gate moved up to allow us entry. Inside were plain walls with supplies on the left and two men in front of us. They wore black clothes with metal vests.

One was smaller and rugged, the other tall and clean cut. Not just tall, he looked like he had eaten a refrigerator. The guy just kept getting larger and larger as Commander Shaw moved inside the garage.

We exited the vehicle, going over to the men.

"Eric, Charles," Commander Shaw said to the men, embracing them like brothers. "It's been much too long."

"It's good to see you again, Shaw," Eric, the smaller of the two said as he embraced the commander. And your friends. Any friend of Shaw's is a friend of mine."

"This is Monica Warden. It's her father we'll be extracting tomorrow night, and our associate Daniel Hunt," Commander Shaw introduced us. "Monica, Daniel, this is Eric and Charles Rasher. They're a brother team we've had here on Mars for many years. They report to us on Immortal Corp movements and the goings on with the Galactic Government here in Elysium."

"It's great to meet you both," Eric said, shaking our hands. He motioned to his larger brother. "My baby brother here doesn't talk much these days. Took some shrapnel in his throat during an incident on the moon, but I'm sure he's happy to meet you as well."

Charles grinned and nodded as he also shook our hands. The guy's palm enveloped my own like I was a little kid. I was grateful he was on our side at least for the time being.

Since X and I figured out the Commander's secret, a feeling of unease was beginning to grow in the pit of my stomach.

"Is everything prepared?" Commander Shaw asked Eric. "Are we still on track to make our move tomorrow night?"

"Affirmative," Eric answered while Charles nodded emphatically. "Rest tonight, plan and prepare tomorrow, then as soon as night falls again, it's go time."

CHAPTER TWENTY-FIVE

THE GARAGE WAS ATTACHED to something that looked more like a penthouse than a safe house. Luxurious rooms, with a massive kitchen stocked with food and beds so soft I swear I sank in a good three inches, welcomed us.

That night, we ate like kings and slept like babies. Maybe I shouldn't have slept so well with a deadly mission staring me in the face the next day, but I couldn't help it.

I gave my body as much rest as it needed, not even getting out of bed until noon. Showers and more food saw me ready and eager early in the afternoon.

Something had been itching at the back of my mind since we touched down in Elysium. It was a thought I couldn't shake, and to be honest, I wasn't sure I wanted to. I was in the same city where Amber had died. The bridge Echo had ambushed her on shouldn't be more than a few minutes' drive.

"X," I asked as I looked out one of the small windows the building had to offer. "The bridge in Echo's memory where he killed Amber, can you locate it here in the city? Do you know where it is?"

"I do," X said after a long silence. "Daniel, when is enough, enough? You saw her die, you forced yourself to live through that again. Do you need to go to the physical site too? Do you need to put yourself through that again?"

"I don't know if I have to, but I feel like I owe her that much for not being there when she needed me the most," I said, as shocked as X must have been at the revelation, not used to talking to anyone about the maelstrom of feelings boiling inside of me. I had to take a moment to pause. I didn't even know I felt that way. I didn't realize how much guilt I carried with me for Amber's death.

"Daniel," X said quietly.

"I wasn't there when she needed me the most," I said. "Where was I, X? Where was I that was more important than by her side? I should have been with her."

"Blaming yourself for the actions of others is a fast road to insanity," X answered. "You can't be everywhere at once. We both know that if you had the inkling of an idea that Amber was in trouble, you would have been right there with her. If you need to go visit the bridge, I'll tell you where it is."

I nodded, still looking out the window in front of me to the street beyond. Only a few vehicles rolled by on the street. Another few took to the air, not by necessity, but rather, leisure.

"It's walking distance," X said, overlapping my field of vision with a small map that popped up in the corner. "Just a kilometer and a half away."

"Thank you," I told her.

I made my way from the room toward the garage where Commander Shaw and Eric were talking.

"I have to do something," I told them. "It won't take long. I'll be back in an hour, two at the most."

Eric looked at the commander with uncertainty in his eyes. He didn't voice his objection, but it was clear to see on his face.

Commander Shaw remained silent for half a beat.

"Daniel, I trust you, what you did for Monica, recapturing Echo and meeting the dropship on time just like you said you would from Cecile, all leads me to believe I made the right decision," Commander

Shaw said with hard eyes. "If you need an hour or two on your own to visit a bridge, I completely understand."

I had forgotten that while I was in Echo's memory, the projectors the scientist wheeled in made the events available for everyone in the room to see. Commander Shaw and Monica knew of the bridge in Elysium where Amber had died.

"Yes, thank you," I said.

"Sir?" Eric looked confused. "Do you think it's wise for one of our members to leave a few hours—"

"It's okay, Eric," Commander Shaw waved me off. "He has to do something. He'll be back."

I left the garage through an exterior door as Commander Shaw explained to Eric what I would be doing. I didn't mind that story was being told. It didn't really matter now.

I walked through the business district of Elysium. I passed very few people on the streets. The flow of traffic was sparse but consistent. A vehicle on the road or in the air would pass me every few seconds.

I followed the route X set out for me with the broken lines charting my course. The lines came over my path in that same golden yellow light I was used to seeing when I activated my night-vision mode.

I passed gorgeous store fronts, clean white and cream buildings, and luxury vehicles the likes of which I had only ever heard about. Mars was truly a refuge for the wealthy.

When we finally reached the bridge, I had to steel my nerves to actually walk over it. I replayed the events in my mind's eye over and over as I crossed the hard path on the right side of the bridge where Amber had died.

I saw Echo ambush her and send her over the edge to her watery grave. I remembered the fire in her eyes. I grinned as I recalled her send her knife into the side of Echo's neck even after being thrown from her vehicle and receiving a barrage of rounds.

The woman had possessed an unquenchable spirit. I imagined that was one of the many reasons I had fallen in love with her.

I finally reached the portion of the bridge where she had been thrown off attached to a thick section of the stone railing.

The railing and any indication of the altercation had been repaired. There wasn't so much as a scratch to remember the event by. That was probably what the inhabitants of Elysium wanted. No stains of the past to muddy their perfect days.

My hands rested on the hard stone railing of the bridge as I stared into the still water of the lake. Not so much as a ripple disturbed the water. If there were fish in the lake, I didn't see any.

"I wonder if they fished her body out?" I asked out loud.

"Public records state they have," X answered. "There's a grave for her under a different name here on Elysium. They buried her under one of her aliases. Would you like me to tell you where?"

"Thanks, but no," I said, staring into the water one last time. "You were right, X."

"About what?"

"About not living in the past only to die in the future," I answered. "I'll never forget her, but right now, it's time to get a handle on these emotions and memories and put them into action. Fuel for the fire."

"Hmmm," X said. "Daniel, I'm not sure that's the healthiest way to deal with this."

"Maybe not, but it's what I have to give at the moment," I said. "The anger inside of me needs an outlet."

"You know I'm with you," X said in a soft quiet voice. I swore I could feel a light pressure on my right shoulder as if she were reaching out to extend a hand of comfort.

"I know, X," I said, turning away from the bridge and back down the way we had come. "Thank you. It's time to make good on a promise now. First we rescue Professor Warden and then we make Immortal Corp bleed for their sins."

CHAPTER TWENTY-SIX

I KNEW my time frame for talking to the commander about his true age was closing. If I was going to do it, I needed to do it now before we prepared and left to go save Monica's father.

Monica and the brothers were in the garage going over supplies and gear needed for the rescue. Commander Shaw was in the living room with a datapad on his lap. A schematic of the building we were about to breach shone, as a hologram, from the piece of tech.

"Commander," I said, seizing the opportunity. "I want you to know that what I'm about to ask you doesn't change how I feel about this mission. I'm still committed to getting Monica's father back. I just need to know something before we go in."

"You want to know how old I am," Commander Shaw said without looking up from his datapad. "Or rather, how I can be so old without looking like it. Is that right?"

I took a step back, narrowing my brow. He was right on the money of course, but how did he know?

"It wasn't that difficult. A matter of time before you knew really," Commander Shaw said, placing the datapad on the glass table in front of him. He leaned back in his seat and skewered me with a pensive stare. "You're not like the others, Daniel. You know that already. Was it that AI that helped tip you off?" he asked. "She's state-of-the-art tech. You're lucky to have her."

"It was X," I answered. "She's helped me out more than a few times."

Commander Shaw nodded slowly. He stared at me for a moment longer as if he were deciding how much he was going to allow himself to say.

"I am much older than I appear," Commander Shaw said after a brief pause. "I'm old enough to have seen the Earth fall, the exodus of mankind to the stars, and now the destabilization of freedom as we know it."

"How?" I asked, already coming to terms with how old this guy really was. "That serum you drink?"

"The serum is just to help my body adjust to the aging process or lack of the aging process, more precisely," Commander Shaw said. "When Phoenix was first established, we knew we needed a leader who would stay the course. The war we fight has been going on for a very long time. To ensure Phoenix never lost sight of that, we decided to rotate our leaders into a hyper-induced state of sleep. When we were needed the most, one of us would be woken to take the reins and ensure Phoenix prevailed."

"How many of the Phoenix leaders are in this hypersleep?" I asked. "When were you awoken?"

"I can't answer your first question," Commander Shaw answered. "I'm willing to make this relationship work but swore an oath to keep the identity and number of the sleeping founders hidden. If our enemies knew what was going on they'd hunt down the other sleeping founders and kill them, thus cutting the head from Phoenix. I can answer your second question however. I was woken when my predecessor went to rest. I took the reins on the super seed project."

"So you're it?" I asked. "All that having to check with your superiors back at the Vault was just for show. You're in charge of Phoenix."

"That's right." Commander Shaw nodded. "For

now, at least. If anything happens to me, another leader will be awoken. If I can pull us out of this mess, then eventually, I'll go back to sleep successful and another leader will take the reins when his or her time comes." Commander Shaw looked thoughtful. He shook his head slowly, looking not at me, but the wall in front of him. "That hypersleep is not what you think. It drags on and on and on for what seems like forever. I don't envy those who are trapped in its cold embrace now."

I gave him a minute before moving on with the list of questions I had for him.

"You saw the Earth fall, you said? That was over a thousand years ago." I did some quick math on the history I had come to know about Earth. "You saw the moon and Mars colonized?"

"I was there when the Order pushed the Earth over the brink and into desperation." Commander Shaw nodded. "I was put into hypersleep then awoken one more time in an hour of great need. Then I was put back into hypersleep and reactivated for the time I lead now."

"That's telling me a lot without really giving me any details," I said.

"I know," Commander Shaw said with a sly smile. "In time, once I feel I can fully trust you, there will be the opportunity for more knowledge. Alternately, if you decide to fight for Phoenix after we save Doctor Warden and make a lasting commitment, I'll be able to divulge more information."

"So what's your mission now?" I asked. "I mean, why were you awoken? To see the super seed project to fruition? To re-terraform the Earth?"

"That was one of the main goals," Commander Shaw said, pursing his lips. "And I think I may have a solution to that problem. Everyone wants the knowledge to bring life back to Earth, maybe even the moon and Mars. They're kidnapping, extorting, and willing to kill for it. So why not just give it to them?"

"You lost me," I said. "I'm sure there's an answer in there somewhere, but you just want to give away the information?"

"That's right," Commander Shaw said with a shrug. "We'll upload it and make the information accessible to everyone. We're not trying to monetize the super seed, so what do we care? If the information is everywhere, there'll be no reason for Immortal Corp, the Order, and whoever else is out there to try and control it. Who knows, maybe some young up and coming billionaire will figure out a way to replicate and manufacture the super seed on a global scale."

I nodded slowly, understanding his plan.

"They can't steal from everyone," I said, scratching the back of my head and thinking of the fallout. "It sounds good in theory."

"I'm sure Earth will be revisited by a new wave of colonists and business owners trying to be the first to market, but that's better than a few shadow organizations killing each other for it," Commander Shaw said. "As far as my age and the fact that I need to hypersleep, I'd like to keep that between you and me. There are only a handful of Phoenix members who know."

"I have no desire to rain on your parade," I told him. "I just needed to clear the air between us before I followed you into the belly of the beast."

"I can respect that," the commander said.

Just then, the door to the garage opened. Monica, Eric, and Charles walked in. The talkative brother was going on about something that had to do with an exotic animal on Mars.

"Really, you've never seen a genetically enhanced Martian dog?" Eric was asking her as if she were from another planet. "They're all the rage here on Mars these days. Genetically altered cats that change colors. Dogs that don't even look like dogs anymore."

"Nope," Monica said with a shrug. "Haven't heard of anything like that. We've been trying to stay alive and focusing on bringing life back to Earth and all."

Charles smiled and nudged his brother.

"Oh, right," Eric said. "Just that kind of stuff."

"I'm glad you all came in," Commander Shaw said, touching a few buttons on his smart pad. A blue holographic image appeared in the air above the tablet. It was the same building I had seen in Echo's memory, the one he took his orders from when he was given Amber's kill order. "This is an image of the building we'll be infiltrating tonight."

Commander Shaw maneuvered around the structure, turning it this way and that with his hands so we could get a full three-hundred-and-sixty-degree view.

"We can expect heavy resistance with as many as eight Immortal Corp soldiers inside," Commander Shaw explained. "We'll have Monica in the vehicle monitoring the local Galactic Government channel while the four of us act as an extraction team."

"With all due respect, sir," Monica said. "It's my father we're going after. I should be going in to help rescue him."

"You lack the required skills needed for a job like this," Commander Shaw told her. "You're a doctor, not an operator. Let us do what we do best. You can still help. We'll need a quick exit and someone to tell us if the Galactic Government has gotten wind of what we're doing here."

Monica buttoned up, but I could tell she wasn't happy.

"We'll act in teams of two," Commander Shaw continued with the explanation of the infiltration. "Eric and Charles, you'll breach the door and secure our exit point. Daniel and I will go into the lab where we anticipate Professor Warden is being held."

It was a simple plan, solid but simple. I didn't see any flaws. The hard truth was the flaws in the plan wouldn't be clear until we were already in it. We'd have to adapt to survive.

"Eric, Charles?" Commander Shaw asked, looking at the brothers. "You two have been monitoring the building since we learned this is where they're keeping the professor. Anything to add?"

"Speed will be our greatest asset here," Eric said, pointing to the side door. "They'll know we're coming as soon as we enter the alley. I can set the charges in eight seconds and blow the door for you to come in right after us. By the time they see us coming and realize what's happening, we should be inside."

Charles used a thick finger to point to the side door and inside the structure. He lifted six fingers and then made a zero shape with his right hand.

"Charles thinks we can be in and out in sixty seconds," Eric translated for his brother. "Any longer and we're risking Immortal Corp calling for reinforcements or the local Galactic Government presence getting reports in and routing a patrol in our direction."

"Sixty seconds from breach to grabbing the professor is going to be tight," I said. "We'll have to be running the entire time. When something goes wrong, we'll have to adjust on the fly and keep moving."

Everyone in the room, even Monica, nodded.

"All right," Commander Shaw broke the silence. "We have our plan. Any gear you need will be in the garage. Let's go free Professor Warden."

CHAPTER TWENTY-SEVEN

I DECIDED to stick with my roots when it came to weaponry. Unlike the battle in Cecile, we needed to move quickly in and out. My MK II would be enough fire power for the job.

I did, however, add a knife and hatchet to my arsenal. I tucked the weapons in my belt. Armor consisted of a heavy metal chest piece of flat black. We were given masks that concealed our entire faces. Strangely enough, we could see through them from our side and breathing was manageable.

My mind went back to the Cyber Hunter I had run into twice, the woman who wore this same kind of mask with the red cross like symbol on her forehead. It seemed like we all had our secrets today, from hypersleep to late-night conversations with the enemy.

Monica took the wheel as we headed away from the safe house to the building where her father was being held. The cold in the air was enough to be able to see your breath by. I ran the plan through my mind over and over again as we traveled in silence. I sat in the row of seats behind Monica and Commander Shaw.

Eric sat next to me with Charles in the back seat. The time of night meant there was little to no traffic on the wide Martian roads. We passed a total of three other vehicles on our way. It was three o'clock in the morning.

The only people that should be out at this time of night were those working night shifts or up to no good. I should know. I was a member of the second group.

We arrived across the street from the building I saw in Echo's memory. The one story structure looked as unassuming as a privately owned caf shop. Anyone walking by would have no idea the nefarious goings on that occurred inside.

"We hit it and we hit it hard," Eric said, unzipping a black duffle bag by his feet. "Give me five seconds lead time then come in running. We should have breached the door right as you arrive. Hit it hard and it'll fall."

"I'll go in first," I said to the commander. "For multiple reasons, I should go in first."

Commander Shaw turned to me with a stiff nod. He pulled the mask gathered at his brow down over his face.

Eric, Charles, and I did the same.

Monica had a mask in case she needed to get out of the vehicle. Right now, there was no point in having her wear it. The van's tinted windows would be cover enough.

"I'll keep the vehicle running," Monica said. "Are you all on the same channel?"

A series of affirmatives answered her.

"I'll let you know if there's the slightest whisper on the Galactic Government channel," Monica said, going over the plan.

"If we don't see you in this world, we'll see you in the next," Eric said, maneuvering to a hunched position right next to the sliding door to the van. "Charles, ready?"

The large man had already pulled his own mask over his face. He shrugged in his chest armor then checked the rifle he carried. It held a long suppressor at the end of the barrel.

Charles looked like something out of a nightmare. I

wouldn't want to go up against the hulking figure without a face. He nodded to his brother.

"Two, one, go," Eric said as calm and cool as ever. With a single smooth move, he opened the van door. In his free hand, he carried the duffle of explosives and sprinted across the street and through the alley.

Charles was a half step behind. The van actually lifted an inch or two as the massive man stepped out and followed his older but smaller brother.

The cold air hit my masked face as I counted to five in my head.

One, two.

Eric and his brother crossed the street and reached the alley.

Three, four.

They were lost to sight a moment later. My heart drummed in my ears. My breathing became quick and excited as adrenaline was unleashed.

Five.

I jumped out of the vehicle, closing the door behind me. I heard more than saw Commander Shaw do the same.

I was across the street and in the alley in a matter of seconds. I pulled the MK II from the holster at my back. The weapon didn't have my fancy drum. My traditional tungsten rounds would have to do tonight.

I saw Eric working on placing the explosives on the door. Charles assumed a protective stance, covering his brother while he worked.

A moment later, Eric maneuvered to a position on the side of the door. Charles did the same. Eric hit a detonator in his hand.

The explosion was short-lived and violent as the explosives detonated around the perimeter of the door like a string of well-placed dominos. The steel door smoked and sparked but didn't fall in.

I struck the door at a dead sprint. My right shoulder took the bulk of the blow as both the door and I fell inward. The hall was just like I had seen in Echo's memory. A pair of Immortal Corp guards were coughing, trying to reorient themselves to what was going on.

When they saw me crash through the door, they lifted their weapons in my direction.

Two pulls of my trigger later, they were down and neutralized as I regained my feet.

Another pair of guards came from a hall on the left.

Commander Shaw was on my right as we took down the pair with a handful of precision shots. Commander Shaw carried a short-barreled rifle that sounded like a deep *thunk* every time he pulled the trigger.

I took the lead, maneuvering over the bodies as I hurried for the door that would lead to the laboratory. I descended the steep flight of steps, taking them two at a time. Speed was the key here, so instead of trying the lock, I just kicked the door in, ready for a fight.

Apparently, our surprise edge was over. A slew of rounds greeted me from four guards on the opposite side of the room. Glass shattered at a dozen different points of contact. I took a round to my chest plate and then my left thigh.

I grunted in pain, going down to a knee. I squeezed my trigger, taking one of the guards in his head and another with a pair of rounds to his chest.

Commander Shaw walked past me with his eye down the sights of his weapon. The man was fearless as he waded into the room under the onslaught of red laser rounds.

His weapon *thunk*ed out laser rounds at a dizzying rate as he took out the first guard then the second. Somehow he remained unscathed.

I wanted to ask him if he had a death wish, but I think I might have answered that question for myself already. The commander didn't seem too enthused about going back into hypersleep. Maybe he was done being put under and brought back. Maybe his ticket out of it all was going down in the fight.

There was no time to debate the state of the commander's suicidal tendencies. He walked across the room, making sure the hostiles were done before coming back to me.

"You going to make it?" he asked, looking down at my bleeding leg.

"I'll live," I said, grimacing as I fought my way back to my feet. Already the pain was subsiding, the bleeding coming to a slow stop.

"He's not here," Commander Shaw said, looking around the large open room only divided with broken glass walls. It was definitely a lab. The army of specialized equipment, from beakers to burners and other tools I could only guess at told us as much. "There was another room in Echo's memory."

"Down the hall, here," I said, following the right side of the room. A hall led to the room where Echo and Sam received their order to kill Amber.

I was less prone to kick this one in. Instead, I reached for the door and turned the knob. It opened. The small room had been converted into a kind of holding cell. There was a bed with a dresser on the right, no windows.

In the middle of the room, Monica's father stood with an Immortal Corp guard holding a firearm to the side of his head. The guard positioned himself behind the professor, barely showing the top of his face.

"Drop your weapons," the guard said in a rush of words. "Drop your weapons. I've already sent the signal out. Reinforcements will be here in minutes. Drop your weapons or I put a laser in the doctor's skull."

I didn't know what the commander was thinking, but I sure as heck wasn't going to lower my weapon.

"X, what are the odds with my training that I can hit that guy in the forehead without hurting the doctor?" I asked.

Everyone in the room, even Commander Shaw, looked at me like I was crazy.

"Hey, I told you I'd kill him!" the guard shouted. "I'm not playing around here. I'll do it! You don't think I'll do it?"

"I thought you never wanted me to tell you the odds?" X asked, using her external speakers.

"Humor me," I said.

"At this range, with your training and the calibration of your weapon, you have a ninety-one point seven five percent chance of neutralizing the guard without causing harm to the professor," X answered. "If you move quickly."

I squeezed the trigger one more time.

The guard holding Monica's father hostage slumped to the ground, motionless. A pool of blood spread out under his body.

"Oh, thank you, thank you." Professor Warden shook as he looked down beside him.

"Let's go," Commander Shaw said, running over to the doctor and helping him from the room.

I knew I should be moving right along with them. We needed to go. There was no update on the Galactic Government from Monica, but I didn't think the dead guard in the room was bluffing. I believed that Immortal Corp reinforcements were on the way.

Being in that room felt like anchors were connected to my feet. The three monitors that stood on the far wall in Echo's memory were gone, but I could see them in my mind's eye as clear as day.

The events of Amber's kill order played back in my mind. The three shadow figures on the screens. The look on Sam's face as she received the news. I remembered it all.

"Daniel, Daniel," X said louder. "We have to go. I get it, it's hard. But we have to go, right now."

X's voice cut through my mental paralysis in a way Monica or anyone else's hadn't. I snapped out of my trance-like state to hear Monica on the other end.

"Daniel, where are you?" Monica was asking in a

rush of words. "Daniel, my father and the commander are out. Eric and Charles are still securing the door. Where are you? Do you need help?"

"No, no, I'm on my way out," I said, running from the room and traveling through the laboratory. "I'm coming."

I sprinted into the hall and out the door to the alley. Eric and Charles welcomed me with quick nods and we were all running down the alley together.

My sixth sense went off like an actual alarm piercing the cold night air. I stopped almost at the same time I heard the voice.

"*Mijo*," the gruff voice called out to me from the night. "Daniel."

I skidded to a stop right before crossing the street.

Eric and Charles did the same, lifting their weapon to try and find the voice.

Commander Shaw and Monica's father were already in the van.

"If I wanted any of them dead, they would be," the voice said from the darkness. "None of this matters anymore, Daniel. None of this matters. Your Phoenix friends can go. We already have what we needed from the doctor. It's time to talk."

A cold sweat beaded across my brow. While Preacher's familiar voice reached my ears, I had pinpointed his location. He was on the roof of the building opposite the secret Immortal Corp installation we had just liberated Monica's father from.

I looked up to see the silhouette of a man with a sword hilt pointed over his right shoulder. I couldn't see much else in the darkness.

Eric and Charles lifted their weapons. They followed my eyes and aimed at Preacher's silhouette.

"No!" I shouted. I extended a hand toward them to tell them to lower their weapons. I knew Preacher was right. He could've already killed them all if he wanted. Probably without breaking a sweat.

My memory of the man was still hazy but somehow I trusted him. Everything inside of me told me this was a man I followed.

"Go," I told the Phoenix team. "Go, your mission is accomplished. I'll find you."

"Daniel," Monica said, pleading with me. "Daniel, come with us."

Two unmarked vehicles skidded around the corner of the street a block away. They sped toward us. Through the front windshield, I could make out the familiar dark uniform of an Immortal Corp soldier.

CHAPTER TWENTY-EIGHT

"GO!" I shouted again as I slapped a new charge pack into the butt of my MK II. I lifted the weapon with both hands, sighting down the barrel. "I'll find you. Go!"

"He's made his choice and now we have to make ours," Commander Shaw shouted. "Monica!"

Eric and Charles were halfway into the van. The appearance of this new threat gave them pause. I shook my head. They took my cue and entered the van, closing the door behind them.

With indecision in her eyes, Monica gunned the engine and sped off down the street.

I walked into the middle of the road, pumping the lead Immortal Corp vehicle with tungsten steel rods. I fired three rounds into the front of the vehicle, sending a plume of smoke into the air. A fire started under the hood. The vehicle spun out of control to the left, crashing into a building headfirst.

I went down to a single knee, aiming at the second vehicle hurtling toward me. A single shot blew out the right front tire, jerking the vehicle to the right. Like its counterpart, it hopped the curb and ran headfirst into the building.

The acrid smell of smoke assailed my nostrils as the light breeze pushed the smoke from the vehicles in my direction.

I heard cursing coming from the occupants as they stumbled out of the vehicles. Four came from the vehicle on the left and four from the one on the right. They lifted their weapons in my direction.

It was clear to see that once these guards exited the vehicle they were unlike the other Immortal Corp guards we had come across thus far. These men and women were dressed in thick armor plates, some combination of fabric and metal I had never seen before. On their heads, there were slender helmets that fit their faces perfectly.

Preacher was so quiet, I didn't even hear him make the jump off the rooftop. The next second, he stood beside me. He looked at the Immortal Corp soldiers streaming out of the vehicles with his one good eye.

"That's enough," he said to them just as much as he said to me.

"Sir?" one of the guards asked in a stressed voice. "We were told the safe house was compromised. We have orders to capture any threat and secure the building."

"Unless whoever gave you those orders ranks higher than me, you have new orders," Preacher said in a tone so hard, there was no room for argument. "Stand down."

The Immortal Corp soldiers looked at one another with grim eyes. Preacher must have seen the same thing I did. These guys had come for a fight and they weren't going home without one.

The four soldiers in each vehicle pointed heavy blasters in our direction. I knew we weren't going to get out of this one unscathed.

"I'll take the vehicle on the left," Preacher said to me just above a whisper. His voice was on the verge of sounding excited for the fight.

There wasn't an agreed upon time for the fight to start or some gentleman's signal that told us the moment for killing was at hand. The street simply erupted in violence.

I sprinted to my right, firing off a few rounds from my MK II. My round struck the enemy, I was sure of that. They did not, however, go down. The force of the rounds jerked their bodies back, but the heavy armor they wore withstood my rounds.

Curses and grunts of pain were the best my MK II could do against whatever kind of armor they wore. On their part, they hosed me with fire as I ran for the safety of a doorway set inside a building to my right.

"Could use some explosives or gas rounds right about now," X said in my head. "Those rounds aren't getting through."

"I know, I know!" I shouted back to her over the sounds of the weapon being discharged.

I snuck a glance from the doorway I took cover behind to see how Preacher was faring.

The man moved like a shadow. He was light on his feet and bounded more than ran toward his grouping of four enemies on the left side of the street. With a single move, his blade was in his hands.

I could see the weapon for what it was now, a katana, expertly made by a true master sword maker. It was an Amakuni, a relic from the old world. How I knew all of this, I had no idea. The blade sparked a memory from my past. I wasn't sure how I knew, but I did know I was right. The weapon in Preacher's hands sparked awe and admiration in my eyes.

Preacher was struck in the torso and shoulder

despite his expert maneuvers in reaching the four Immortal Corp soldiers. The hits barely dazed him as he reached his opponents and began slashing at their armor.

I took in all of this in a matter of seconds. There wasn't time to watch. I would have loved to watch Preacher work with that iconic weapon in his hands. The four heavily armored guards on my side of the street turned their attention to Preacher as the screams of those he tore asunder filled the night air.

I mentally prepared myself for my own run. My MK II wasn't getting the job done. I'd have to get up close and personal. I checked the blade and axe at my belt then slowed my heartbeat.

I saw the action in my mind of me making the run toward the enemy and landing among them just like Preacher had done.

Then all the time for thinking and planning was over. I turned the corner and took off at a sprint. They were ten meters in front of me, taking cover behind the smoking vehicle as they aimed at Preacher and started taking shots.

I caught movement from the corner of my eye as Preacher used the katana as an extension of his own body. Unlike my MK II, his katana was having little trouble slicing through their armor.

I swore the blade hummed and glowed a dull red as it cut through both armor and flesh. Questions about the weapon would have to wait. Thanks to the distraction Preacher created, I was able to make the run without being hit, in a matter of seconds.

I vaulted over the vehicle the four guards on my side of the street used for cover. I unloaded my MK II clip into the first Immortal Corp soldier at point blank range.

I was so close, I actually pressed the barrel of the weapon against the center chest piece of my opponent. Even the high tech armor was no match for the hand cannon at such a close range. The rounds went through, sending one of the soldiers slumping to the ground.

The other three Immortal Corp guards turned in my direction, aiming their weapons at me. Instinct more than anything else lifted my knife from its resting place in my belt. The first target, I struck in the throat with a quick jab from my left hand. I maneuvered around him to use his body as a shield against the incoming fire from the other two.

I used my free hand to rip the helmet he wore upward and plant my blade in the base of his skull.

He went wobbly-legged as he breathed his last. I bullied him forward into the incoming fire of the other two guards. Shoving the dying man into one of the soldiers, I went after the other.

I batted my next target's hand away as he tried to point his weapon around his dying comrade. I struck out as hard as I could with the bottom of my right foot. The strike landed on the man's left knee, forcing him down as cartilage and ligaments tore and snapped.

He let out a cry of pain before I snapped his neck with a violent, short-lived jerk.

"Daniel, look out!" X warned out loud.

The last guard shoved the dying man in his arms away and lifted a pulse rifle to the side of my head.

I was caught. He had me dead to rights. I had taken too long with the third enemy, as short as it seemed. I was a half second too late.

This is going to hurt, I thought to myself as I prepared for the rounds to strike the side of my skull.

They never did.

As if by magic, the hilt of a sword sprouted from the Immortal Corp guard's chest. The blade glowed a beautiful red color, going through the armor as if it weren't there at all.

The guard looked down at the sword sticking out of his chest as if he couldn't believe it either. His weapon fell to the ground as his hands hit his sides. He sank to his knees then keeled over.

I was breathing hard, still coming off the adrenaline dump. Preacher ran over, pulling his sword free from the Immortal Corp guard's chest.

The weapon hummed as if it were activated by his touch. I was so close to it now I could see it did in fact glow with a dull red light. Preacher pressed something on the hilt of the weapon.

The blade lost its glow, reverting back to gunmetal steel. He cleaned the blade reverently then placed it back in its sheath behind his shoulder.

He was wounded both in his torso and shoulder. Dark bloody spots showed through his clothing. I was going to ask him if he was going to be all right, but that seemed silly.

I knew what he was just as much as I knew myself.

"Why didn't they stand down?" I asked. "You still work for the same organization, right? They don't take orders from you?"

"They knew who I am, but the Pack operates apart from the rest of Immortal Corp. We're like the shock troops while the guards are your normal infantry. They had orders, so they did what they felt they had to do. We did the same."

In the distance, the familiar wail of sirens permeated the cold night air. It seemed our luck was finally up. Even in this deserted business section of town, someone had seen or heard enough to call in the local praetorians.

The sounds of the approaching Galactic Government forced me into movement. I cleaned my own knife and holstered my MK II.

"Let's clear out," Preacher said, turning to look at me. A shadow of a grin rested on his lips. "We're done here. It's true, you really don't remember, do you?" Preacher asked with a tilt of his head. "Danny, it's good to see you. I wish it was under better circumstances, but we have to go. Do you trust me?"

"Trust is a strong word," I told the man I so desperately wanted to remember. "But I'm willing to have a conversation."

"Good enough for me," Preacher said as the wails of the sirens grew. "We better have that conversation somewhere else or we'll be in cuffs taken downtown. Follow me."

I obeyed, taking in the destruction we left in our wake. Eight guards equipped in the latest armor, well trained and lethal in their own right, lay dead on the ground. Preacher had taken a pair of shots, and me, nothing.

I shuddered, thinking of what two members of the Pack could do. Sam and I had taken out a small army. If there had been a total of seven members in our original pack, what had we been able to accomplish together? Seven near immortal beings trained to fight and enhanced to kill.

Maybe the better question was what weren't we able to do. I could imagine a scenario where we were created to take on an entire army. Give the Galactic Government a run for their money in a guerilla-style war even.

I walked behind Preacher as these thoughts ran through my mind. We made our way down the street away from the safe house and the approaching sirens. Preacher wove his way through a few city streets. Finally, he slowed his pace as the sirens began to fade. A large park sprawled out in front of us. Sand crunched under our feet. Everywhere, there were carefully carved sculptures. To our right, a small lake; to the left, equipment for children to play on.

The hour was still so early, there was no one in sight. My breath made puffs of steam in front of my face.

"I have transportation on the other side of the park," Preacher said to me. He lost some of the hard edge to his tone. "We'll cut through and be out of here before the Galactic Government ever gets sight of us. We have a lot to talk about, Daniel. I'm glad you're back."

EPILOGUE

PREACHER'S APARTMENT was deceptive in that it was in the nicest, tallest building in the downtown area but looked like it was vacant on the inside. It didn't seem decorating was high on his priority list. The kitchen and living area had no tables, chairs, or even a rug to bring comfort from the plain cement floors.

What he did have was an amazing view of the city of Elysium. Glass windows acted as walls to my left beside the kitchen and in front of me against the space designated as a family living area.

Preacher unhooked the sword attached to his back and placed it on the marble countertop.

"You still take your caf black?" Preacher asked me, heading to a machine on his counter.

"Still do," I said. I didn't need any more confirmation that I could trust this man, but if I did, there it was. He knew me so well, he knew how I took my caf.

The single memory I had of us working together on a mission was enough for me to go off of. If he wanted to try and kill me, he could have a dozen times by now.

Preacher came over to me with a pair of steaming cups of caf. He handed me one and motioned me over to the window.

The sun was just beginning to rise. The orange globe cast brilliant rays of light over the waking city. We stood there, each lost to his own thoughts, sipping on our steaming cups.

I had a million questions I wanted answered, but something told me to wait. Preacher was about to unravel something big. I could sense it in the man's stance; his hesitancy to speak nearly promised as much.

"It's beautiful, isn't it?" Preacher asked, looking out over the city. "The greatest achievement of mankind. We colonized Mars and it's everything I could have imagined."

"It's something, all right," I said.

"It's what we fight to protect," Preacher said, taking in a long deep breath. "I want you to know I didn't have anything to do with her death. I didn't know. I would have tried to stop it if I had."

"I believe you," I said.

"I looked for you for as long as I could, but you were just gone," Preacher said, turning to take me in. "I thought you were dead. Killed yourself from grief or went out in some kind of blaze of glory. I didn't know."

"That makes two of us," I said back to him. "I'm recovering a lot of my memory, but I still don't know how I lost it in the first place."

"It'll come to you," Preacher said. "In the meantime, I'm glad you're back in the game. There's something that's happened that's changed everything."

Preacher's tone that had been hard-edged and no nonsense softened now. He took in a deep breath, looking me up and down.

"*Mijo*, what I'm about to tell you comes with no obligation to help," Preacher started. Each word was halting, as if he were physically having to push the words past his lips. "There's a fight coming, a fight we may not be able to win. Super seeds, the Order, Phoenix all mean nothing compared to what's at our doorstep."

"Is that why you just let Professor Warden go?" I asked.

"He doesn't mean much anymore," Preacher said with a nod. "He gave us the information we need, but that's not what I'm talking about now."

Preacher took another heavy sigh. He shook his head from side to side. I could see the war waging behind his one good eye.

"By now, you must know the history behind the Order," Preacher asked in more of a question than a statement.

"The Knights Templar, the illuminati," I answered.

"That's right," Preacher said. "Now do you know the origin behind Immortal Corp?"

The question stunned me for a moment. I knew a lot about the company that created me, but I didn't know the true origin of the enemy I fought. With the rivalry against the Order, I imagined Immortal Corp was founded to combat them, but I didn't know.

"I don't," I said. "I know Immortal Corp hates the Order and the other way around."

"That's right," Preacher said. "That rivalry goes back further than anyone can remember. Immortal Corp's name has also changed through the pages of history. Immortal Corp has been around for a long time. They were founded on the doctrine of protecting mankind."

"They have a strange way of protecting," I said,

thinking of how many deaths they must have been responsible for. Of how many deaths they were responsible for just in my short time of getting to know them.

"They have a lot of flaws in their system," Preacher said, actually agreeing with me. "Trust me, I've gone back and forth on whether it's all worth it. How many lives killed justify how many lives saved? We kill one to save ten, is that fair? One to save one? Where do you draw the line, or is there no line to be drawn at all anymore?"

I clammed up. I was the last person to form an answer to this question. How many people had I killed working for Immortal Corp? How much innocent blood was on my hands? How much blood on my hands since I realized what was going on? Sure I could justify it, but a life was a life.

What chilled me even more was the fact that I was prepared to keep taking lives. I'd kill my way to the top until I gave Amber's death meaning and found all my answers along the way.

"Immortal Corp started off as a band of assassins." Preacher picked up the story. "Assassins who swore to protect men against threats both domestic and —alien."

There was no denying that the way Preacher said

the word "alien," he meant to add extra emphasis to it. I searched his one bright blue eye for meaning.

"Alien?" I repeated the word.

"Whispers, rumors, fake news have hinted at us not being alone in the universe for quite a while now, but we have proof," Preacher said, setting his jaw. "I've seen them, Daniel. I've seen them, and unless we find some way to band together, humanity has no chance against them. Nothing, none of this will matter if there is no mankind to go back to Earth, to try and stop the fighting to find answers. It'll all be over."

"How, where?" I asked as my mind tried to bring rational thought to an impossible scenario.

"We might as well have sent signal flares to the galaxy when we left Earth and then colonized the moon and Mars." Preacher took another long swig of his caf. "And even that is only speculation. We won't really know until we can capture and interrogate one of them. What we do know is that they're growing in force and it's only a matter of time before they come for us. They'll take Mars first, then the moon and Earth will follow."

"How much time do we have?" I asked. "Who else knows?"

"Knowing and believing are two different questions," Preacher answered. "The Galactic Government is turning a blind eye, pretending it isn't real. Phoenix is too wrapped up in their super seed and bringing life back to Earth. The Order, well, who knows what they know. I'm not counting on them to partner with us in any case."

"How much time?" I asked, still trying to wrap my head around the fact that we were talking about real life aliens.

"Not enough," Preacher said, draining his cup of caf. "Not enough. They're building a forward base on the opposite side of Mars. They'll use that as a staging ground for the invasion. By the time they conquer Mars, it'll be too late for the forces on the moon to make a stand. Earth goes next."

I finished my own cup, walking away from Preacher and feeling angry.

"So, what?" I asked, not bothering to mask my frustration. "You want me to help you, is that it? You want me to come to the rescue of Immortal Corp? It's because of them that I'm on this path. They killed Amber for no other reason than she wanted a different way. I'm just supposed to forget all of that and go fight your aliens?"

"I'm not saying it's fair or that it even makes sense," Preacher said with a weary sigh. He hunched his shoulders, defeated for a moment. In that brief window, I saw him for what he really was. He was tired.

Preacher had to be twenty to thirty years older than me. Wrinkles showed easily on his face. His grey and white hair and short beard added to the fact that he was old enough to be my father.

"I'm not asking you to forgive Immortal Corp. Hell, I want to kill a few of them myself," Preacher said, straightening his back. "I'm tired of fighting too, but soldiers don't get the choice of when to or when not to fight. Right now, if we sit by and do nothing, then humankind falls. I can't have that. I won't have that. Put that hate in your heart on pause. We can't do this on our own. We'll need everyone to help if we're going to get through this alive."

I rubbed my eyes, trying to figure out what to do next. How could I do anything else but help? If Preacher hadn't gone crazy and he was telling the truth, then we were all going to die unless we did something.

"Seeing is believing," Preacher told me as I stood at his kitchen counter at a loss for words. "I can take you there before you make a decision. You can see for yourself what we're up against. If that's not enough to convince you, you can go about your way. Just see for yourself. I can get us transportation to the uncolonized side of Mars. We can be there in a day's time."

"Okay, okay," I said, resigning myself to the idea that not only did aliens exist but that I would be working with the very company I swore to defeat. "You should know that I'm still coming after them. I mean, the heads of Immortal Corp. The three figures on the screen that gave Amber's kill order."

"And I won't stop you," Preacher said. "Loyalty to Immortal Corp is something that died when they killed one of our own. What I do now goes much further than loyalty. It goes to the preservation of our very species."

DANIEL HUNT WILL BE BACK in the next book in the *Forsaken Mercenary Series, Fury*. Until then, stay informed by **joining our Pack** in the "Jonathan's Reading Wolves" Facebook group and get the latest news on the project.

STAY INFORMED

Get A Free Book by visiting Jonathan Yanez' website.

You can email me at jonathan.alan.yanez@gmail.com or find me on Facebook and Instagram (@author_jonathan_yanez). I also created a special Facebook group called "Jonathan's Reading Wolves" specifically for readers, where I reveal new cover art, do giveaways, and run contests. Please check it out and join whenever you get the chance!

For updates about new releases, as well as exclusive promotions, join the VIP mailing list. Head there now to receive a free copy of *Inception*.

jonathan-yanez.com

Enjoying the series? Help others discover the beginning of the *Forsaken Mercenary* series by sharing with a friend.

BOOKS IN THE FORSAKEN MERCENARY UNIVERSE

Inception

Dropship

Absolution

Fury

Vendetta

Annihilation

Nemesis

Rivals

Wolves

Crusade

Traitor

Parabellum

Judgment

www.ingramcontent.com/pod-product-compliance
Ingram Content Group UK Ltd.
Pitfield, Milton Keynes, MK11 3LW, UK
UKHW040754020326
11004UKWH00042B/588